About the Author

I was not a confident child. I found escape in books, always on the outside of peers, but content in the worlds I could explore in my own comfort. Perhaps my story can bring comfort to someone out there, bring a reminder of why books are so important for those of us on the sidelines—we can see ourselves in books, but we can also learn about ourselves through them too.

Eyes of Violet

Toni Langley

Eyes of Violet

Olympia Publishers
London

www.olympiapublishers.com
OLYMPIA PAPERBACK EDITION

A CIP catalogue record for this title is
available from the British Library.

ISBN: 978-1-80074-467-7

This is a work of fiction.
Names, characters, places and incidents originate from the writer's
imagination. Any resemblance to actual persons, living or dead, is
purely coincidental.

First Published in 2023

Olympia Publishers
Tallis House
2 Tallis Street
London
EC4Y 0AB

Printed in Great Britain

Dedication

To Mama, I'm sorry I was born backwards, but look what I
did! To Dad, thanks for playing Ninja Turtles with me, but
you still owe me a game! And to the Little Three, who will
always be the Little Three no matter how old you get— stop
growing. It's rude to be taller than your big sister.

Acknowledgements

Thank you to eleven-year-old me, for that terrible, *terrible* first draft that started all this—it is locked away, never to be seen again, but I appreciate your effort.

Chapter One

"It's not on!"

It is.

"Is not."

What's that red light, then?

(Pause).

"Decoration."

Just... let me do it.

"No, no! My sister, my story!"

My tape recorder, my story.

"Who has a tape recorder nowadays anyway? Use your phone, Grandad." (Pause). "OK, so he's going to kill me. I will—is this definitely on?" (Loud, raspberry noise, distorted by nearness to mic. There's a sigh in the background). "My name is Ashton. I am devilishly handsome and capture the hearts of all I meet—"

This is why we can't have nice things, Ash. Your ego gets in the way.

"Tape recorders don't capture visual information, *Grandad.* I'm setting the scene."

Give.

"No!"

Just give, I'll do it. (Slight scuffle sound, Ashton blows another raspberry. The second voice becomes clearer, successful in their endeavour of acquiring the tape recorder). "OK, I apologise on behalf of my—"

If you say anything other than husband, I'm divorcing you.

"We're not married."

Not yet!

"Just… give me ten minutes and then you can dolly about with… whatever you do." (Silence. Ashton may be dead). "He's not dead," the second speaker clarifies, "he's sulking. Ash only goes quiet when he's sulking. This is a recording of *our* story and yes, it's on a tape recorder because of aesthetic reasons. Our story starts with Ashton's sister, Violet. She was almost ten—"

Just say nine.

"—and I didn't have a constant migraine as I had not yet met this so-called devilishly handsome, egotistical idiot."

Heart-capturer, Ashton corrects in the background. *Future husband. Future divorcee if you keep giving me attitude.* (Second speaker sighs and is quiet while they count to ten).

"Right. This all started—"

Once upon a time!

"*This. All. Started.*" (Glare). "When Violet was born."

I was born first.

"You're, like, twelve years older than her."

Physically.

"There isn't a low enough number for your mental age."

Rude! (Another raspberry. Another sigh.)

"Anyway…"

***

Ashton was the eldest of the Yachtman kids, followed by a

sister, two brothers and two more sisters, twins. He liked to argue that he was the best-looking and smartest of the bunch, but you, dear reader, will get used to such bold claims.

At the start of this story, Ashton was in his early twenties, still lived at home with his parents – buying a *house* in *this* economy? You must be joking! – and his small army of siblings: Rose, Marv, Killian and the twins, Daisy and Violet. Violet was the youngest, over a decade his junior, but of all his siblings, he connected with Violet the most.

She was a small girl, with the same pale freckled skin he had, the same mad, ginger hair and the same moss-green eyes. She seemed quite ordinary, a little shy, rather tentative, but with a penchant for stealing his chocolate, as all little sisters tend to do.

But from birth, she had always been different.

No one really knew why she had been born like this. It proved quite troublesome for their father.

David Yachtman was a proud man, strong-willed and even stronger tempered. With his dark hair, pressed, tailored suits and a decided set to his jaw, he was *the* man of authority. It came as no surprise to anyone when he built his career up, over and over, until he founded and became the head of the AMCD. The Anti-Mutant Control Department.

That's where Violet came in. At the time of her birth, David had commanded the AMCD for just over a decade, renowned for his prowess, his iron fist and his mercilessness against the mutant infestation. Mutants were creatures that, in most cases, looked every inch a human. But they had powers and abilities of all descriptions and potency, and they were a threat. It wasn't until Violet started exhibiting powers of her own, that David realised – after all these years of quashing mutants underfoot, sometimes literally – his daughter had been born, inexplicably and unforgivably, a mutant.

No one knew. Only her siblings and her parents. Beyond that, it was forbidden. Her being the way she was, was a conundrum, a disgrace. She was a dirty mark on his pristine record. David made sure she knew that.

***

Ashton sketched over the lines, brow furrowed in concentration. He rendered an A-line pleated skirt, but he had misdrawn the waistline. It was nothing fancy, a simple swirl of foliage and daisies along the hem. However, he *had* added in concealed pockets, pockets large enough for the wearer to put their hands in. He never understood why women's clothes didn't have pockets, but babies' clothes did. Seemed a bit backwards, really.

It took him another three tries to get the band around the waist just right. He spun in his chair with a flourish, grinning and proudly showing off his sketchbook. "*Ta-da!*"

"Yay!" Violet contributed, sitting cross-legged on the floor, clapping. He bowed his head.

"Ah, thank you, thank you, too kind!"

She held her hands out. Ashton happily passed the sketchbook over. "How do the colours feel to you?"

Violet squinted at the drawing. There was a crash in the hallway, followed by Marv's cackle of a laugh.

"No fair!" Killian protested.

"Last one downstairs smells bad!"

"No!"

"You need pink." Violet's tiny voice called Ashton's

14

attention back. "Peach. Orange." She drummed her fingers on the paper, silently debating. "Soft orange." She settled with. Ashton smiled and she returned the sketchbook.

"Soft orange it is," he agreed. "OK then."

He set the sketchbook on the desk, turning back to her and folding his arms across his knees. "Let's see yours."

Violet looked down, rubbing her thumb across her finger. She had borrowed some of his stationery, now assembled before her rather haphazardly. Ashton remained quiet while she considered each item, eyes narrowing distastefully at the eraser.

She picked the pencil, biting the inside of her cheek. For a moment, nothing happened. Ashton watched the pencil too, fingers digging into his elbows.

The pencil twitched. Rolled left, then right, like an indecisive baby. The rubber side tilted up, dropped and bounced on the carpet.

Violet curled her hands into her sleeves. The pencil rose, an inch, then two, rotating in the air slowly on its axis. She left it there, gradually turning her focus to the short, Digimon ruler. It hopped once, twice, skittishly flipping over to hide the stickered side. Violet stared at it, offended. Her demand shifted wholly to the ruler. It ignored her. The pencil fell with a soft *ba-bump*.

Ashton beamed at her. "Getting better, Vi!" He leant down, snatching something up lightning quick. "Another few years and you may even lift," – he brandished his prize between thumb and forefinger – "the accursed rubber!" He shoved it in her face, circling it, 'oohing' for dramatic effect. Violet blinked at the Digimon rubber (he had the whole set), and then looked at him. "Pfft." He let the rubber fall. "Tough crowd." Violet gave a little 'mmph', fingers touching her nose – bleeding, again. As it always did after trying to move things.

Gravel crunching startled them, disturbed by the weight of a returning car. "It's all right, Vi." Ashton winced a smile, scooping together his sketchbooks. He kicked out a box from beneath his desk, dumping in it his pile of work. Violet's hands shook, her left tending to the nosebleed, the right clumsily tossing the stationery into the box. Outside, the car door slammed.

Tidied, Ashton pushed the box towards her. She scrambled to hide it in the wardrobe while he wrenched open his desk drawers, talking over his shoulder as he did. "You came in here for a bit of peace and quiet, OK?" he said, slinging out maths books, graph paper and a scattering of non-Digimon stationery. "Here." He flicked a packet of tissues at her without looking around, searching for his calculator.

They froze upon hearing the front door open. Ashton turned stiffly to Violet, ushering her back with a fragile smile and a gentle wave. She stumbled a step, sinking onto the window seat.

"I'm home!" David called. Violet flinched, squashing a wad of tissues to her nose.

"It's OK, Vi," Ashton soothed her, sitting carefully at his desk. "It's OK."

She pressed her lips together, staring out the window, free hand hidden in her sleeve.

Footsteps on the stairs. Ashton opened his textbook to a random page, picking up a pencil and tapping the rubber end in pretence of thinking.

The top step creaked. Violet hiccupped, tucking her chin to her chest.

Their father let himself in. He flung the door open, grasping the handle as though he intended to rip it off. Ashton glanced up, forcing a smile.

Of his six children, the two in this room were the only ones that shared none of his physical features. His slate-grey eyes slid around the room, his dark hair ashine with expensive product, not a strand out of place. He straightened his tie, giving a small, pointed cough.

"Violet," he said, giving a smile that was never a smile. "Why are you here, beast?"

"It's qui—" Ashton began. David's glare cut to him, freezing the remnant of his sentence in his throat.

"You," David said, teeth gritted, corner of his mouth twitching, "have work to do."

"But—"

David took a step forward. Ashton recoiled.

"You *dare* jeopardise your future for *that*?" He flung a repulsed point at the girl. Ashton bit his lip, watching his father's curl into a sneer. "You continue to disappoint me, Ashton."

"She just wanted some quiet time." Ashton pressed on carefully, his voice just above a mumble. "She hasn't bothered me."

His father scoffed. Ashton's hands twitched, resisting the urge to bundle into fists.

He met David's eyes. "Remember what happened the last time she didn't get any quiet time?"

A grunt. That was the only response he received: a non-committal, dismissive grunt.

David turned away from him, marching three steps across the room. Violet squeaked as he snatched hold of her arm,

17

fingers digging in. With a single yank, he wrenched her to her feet; she dropped the bloodied tissues in terror.

David saw them.

"A nosebleed," he said, his tone somehow both light and flat, "why do you have a nosebleed, Violet?"

She stared resolutely at the floor, fighting to quell the tremble in her lower lip. Her shoulders hunched, head down. His grip tightened; she could feel it on her bone. "You've disobeyed me." David answered his own question in that same airy way, a sharp gleam twisting through his eyes.

Ashton rose, a defence on his lips. David snarled, throwing out his hand and striking his son on the chest. Ashton fell from the shove, wheezing, back into his chair.

"No!" Violet pleaded, grasping the hand that held her.

"Don't touch me!" he raged, lashing out. Violet hit the floor, the room see-sawing around her, a throbbing in her cheek. "You vile little freak!" He towered over her; she could see her face in his shoes as he stepped on her fingers. "I let you *live,*" he reminded her in a low growl, "show some respect." The sentence finished with a hiss, as he shifted his foot.

Violet bit back a whimper, tasting blood on her lower lip. She ducked her head, seeing tears stain the carpet. He moved his foot again, like crushing a cigarette butt. Pain splintered up her wrist, bones audibly breaking.

Then Ashton, launching himself forward. Both hands struck David in the chest, knocking him back two steps. Violet watched her brother's feet plant themselves in front of her, one blue sock, one green. *It's a choice,* he had once told her. *I like odd socks.*

She squeezed her eyes shut. Ashton's watch ticked on the dresser. David's shirt crinkled as he pulled it taut at the hem, his need for an impeccable appearance taking priority. Her heart thumped in her ears and her hand. She didn't want to look. She couldn't.

Someone's phone buzzed downstairs. It was happening again. She curled her uninjured hand. A tap dripped in the bathroom. The light bulb hummed. She had to stop this. A bird trilled its song three gardens to the left. A sob caught in her throat, falling into a feeble cough. A whack of flesh on flesh. Lava danced and broiled behind her eyes. Something twisted in the back of her shirt, the world spinning into a vortex.

Cold washed over her skin as she was thrown, the carpet burned her forearm and cheek. A door slammed shut behind her, ricocheting in her skull like a detonated bomb. The sound flooded white-hot across her vision. A lock clicked; her fingers screamed; the tap still dripped; the bird still sang. David was shouting.

Each noise was a knife in her brain. Each knife brought with it a colour, loud and flashing and bright, until all she could hear was a pool of unending cacophony. When the shadows of unconsciousness edged in, Violet welcomed them.

Chapter Two

Dinner was underway when Ella Yachtman came home. She was a midwife on her third late shift of the week but the duress did not stop her from announcing her return in a vibrant singsong voice. Her keys clattered on the bureau; her shoes thumped softly against the wall as she finally kicked them off, and her coat flashed blue over the banister.

"I'm *starving*," she complained good-naturedly, coming in with a smile. "What have we—? *Ash!* What happened to your face?"

Her smile melted with concern as she hurried to her eldest. Her fingers were calloused but soft as she felt his jawline, examining the deep, purple-black bruise staining his cheek and surrounding the skin under his eye. "I can't feel any breaks, but my God, what *happened*?"

"He was jumped," David supplied calmly, cutting into his roast beef. "On the way home from work, right, Ashton?" Grey eyes settled on his son's face.

"From work?" Ella echoed. "I thought you had the day off?"

She gently patted around his eye with her thumb, apologising when he winced.

"Extra shift," he mumbled.

David smirked at him. His wife didn't notice, still examining her son's face.

"I've handled it already," David assured her when she

finally turned to him in question. "I have my best men on the case."

"Aww." She smiled again, hand on heart with relief. "Thank you, love."

She kissed his temple as she passed, moving into the kitchen to collect her dinner. She hummed with the microwave, tapping her fingers on the counter.

Ashton focused on his dinner. He hated beef, thought it the meat variation of cardboard. Beside him, Killian flicked peas at Marv. Rose tutted, breaking apart her Yorkshire pudding. Daisy sat next to her, pouring more gravy onto her plate. She was nothing like Violet, taking after their mother with fair, curly hair and brown eyes the colour of freshly dug earth, inquisitive and proud. Should you ask her, there would be no admitting she had a twin sister.

Ella bustled back in, swinging a chair in beside Ashton, presenting him with half a bag of peas, frozen and wrapped in a tea towel. "Put that on there," she instructed kindly. "Are you eating all right, sweetie? Any pain?"

"No pain; I'm OK."

"Did they take anything? The muggers." She clarified at his blank look.

"His phone." David interrupted. "Hope you had insurance on that thing."

He shovelled vegetables into his mouth, meeting Ashton's eyes levelly. Ashton glared at his plate, the handle of his knife cutting into his palm.

"Mum, Killian won't stop throwing food at me!"

"Mum, Marv won't stop having a target for a face!"

"Boys, I have had a very, very long twelve-hour shift, three days running. I would appreciate being able to eat my dinner without peas in my hair."

"Yes, Mum."

"Sorry, Mum."

"Thank you."

Ashton set his cutlery down a few minutes later, leaving most of his beef soaking up gravy. Ella was listening to Daisy talk about her school project. Rose kicked Killian under the table, shooting him a *behave* look. Killian carefully lowered his forkful of peas and Marv peeked through a gap between his arms, wary of incoming dinner. David was using the last of his Yorkshire pudding to mop up gravy from his plate.

There was no empty seat at this table. No place an extra plate could be set. This, as far as they were concerned, was family dinnertime. Nothing was amiss.

Ashton helped clear the table, left Rose and Marv to wash and dry up. He gave his excuses – work to do, behind on something or other – skipping the creaky, top step.

Violet's room was the last door on the left, beside the bathroom. It wasn't even a room, just a converted crawl space.

It took a paperclip and a hair slide to pick the lock again. Ashton tested the handle, opening the door slowly.

"It's me," he whispered. "Got you some food." He stuck his head in.

Downstairs, Killian was bickering with Daisy—he wanted to watch *Lord of the Rings*. She wanted to watch *Beauty and the Beast*.

Violet's room was narrow—he could hold his elbows out on either side of him and touch both walls. Said walls were slathered improperly with cheap, flaking, off-white paint. A bare lightbulb hung dead from the ceiling. No curtains, but also no windows for curtains to be needed. She had an old cot-bed mattress on the floor, perhaps the one Ashton himself had as a baby.

He found her sitting on this, her back to the wall, facing the door. Red and bleary-eyed, sniffling. She had been curling her hair around her finger, causing it to frizz and poof. Upon the door opening, she stopped, laying her hands in her lap. The left hand she kept suspended, bruised and swollen so, any pressure was too much to bear. Ashton shut the door behind him. "Mind if I sit?"

She glanced at him, a split-second study, before looking down, providing a motion between a nod and a shake. He set a bottle of water and the plate of cold beef sandwiches he had managed to steal next to her.

"He hit you."

"Muggers, apparently."

"I'm sorry."

"It's not your fault." He sat cross-legged on the floor, knees against the end of the mattress.

Violet sniffed.

"Always my fault." She drew her right hand out, poking the sandwich tentatively. "Beef," she mumbled.

"Yeah," he sighed, "I'm not a fan either." She wrinkled her nose. "You need to eat," he prompted. She grimaced at the notion, picking the sandwich up with her right hand, albeit only by her fingertips.

He watched her pick the crusts off one-handed, pinching the layer off with her thumb and forefinger, clumsily rotating it in her palm. Her left hand did not move. He could hear the familiar Disney theme song through the floorboards. "I'll try and get something for your hand."

"He'll know."

23

"He always knows. But I'll still try."

She peeked into her sandwich, scratching her ear on her shoulder. Her eyes flicked to his face, misery dulling the green. "Sandwich," he urged, clicking his tongue when she made another face.

"Fussy old grandma," she muttered, taking small bites. Ashton helped himself to the crusts, seeing the usual flash of guilt in her expression in his periphery. He offered a smile, half-hearted.

Her attention slid to something past his left ear. "You're blue." She picked at her lip. "You're sad."

"Yes, I'm sad."

"Because he hit you?"

"No. Because I want us to get out of here."

"Can't."

"We will one day."

"How?"

"I'm... still working that one out."

"More blue."

"I am?" he asked.

She hummed, nodding, nibbling at the bread. Not so coordinated with her right, fingers shaking, grip fickle on her 'meal'. Ashton thought for a moment, brushing breadcrumbs from his shirt. "What's the opposite of blue?"

She pondered that while she ate the last of her sandwich. She held her water bottle still between her knees to get the lid off, swigging a mouthful to try to swill away the beef taste.

"Soft orange," she decided.

"I'll be soft orange then." He nodded. She narrowed her eyes at him, and he gave a gentle laugh. "Not now. But when we get out of here. I'll be soft orange."

"I like soft orange."

"Me too."

***

Violet woke to the lock clicking open. The hallway light spilt in, blotted with an all-too-familiar shadow. She lay perfectly still, watching the shadow move closer on her wall through half-closed eyes. Fought to keep her breathing even, to keep up the pretence of sleep, in the hope that it would deter him.

It never did.

Her father grabbed her arm, fingers burrowing into the bruises the very same digits had caused earlier.

"Up," David growled. She didn't move fast enough, his fist coming down, splattering white stars of pain through her head.

Dazed, she was yanked to her feet. Her stomach flip-flopped with nausea, bile pooling at the base of her throat. She was hauled along the landing. She reached for Ashton's door, but David was too quick for her. His rough hand clamped around her broken fingers quicker than she could blink, the other over her mouth to catch her yelp. He shushed her. She could see his smile in her peripheral vision, swallowing sick, eyes burning.

Down the stairs, to the cupboard door beneath them. He produced a key from his pocket, the only one of its kind and one she was all too familiar with.

The door swung open. He hauled her in. It was not ordinary storage space, not with David Yachtman holding the key. Stone steps into a whitewashed stone basement, as perpetually cold as a winter's morning. Her breath fogged

25

before her face. She knew every inch of this room: the expanse of monitors on the right-hand wall, the army of chalkboards and whiteboards on the left with ever-changing workings on it. In the middle was a maze of desks and lab counters, almost buried under computers, folders, vials, tools and AMCD equipment. Handcuffs that administered a fatal, excruciating poison at the smallest display of power. Prods packed with enough voltage to stop a human heart, enough to temporarily paralyse a mutant. And crowns. He called them crowns, grinning at her with a sadism that turned her nerves to cold lightning. It was a headband, really, that encircled the head and covered the eyes, made of alloys and wires and components she did not understand but had helped in creating. She was the lab rat to his crowns. Mind-reading devices, designed to wring out every thought, every movement, every feeling from the victim until their brain fried in their skull. "I've not given you its full ability," David often told her, patting the invention proudly, "you have nothing I want to know."

Nothing he wanted to know in her brain, perhaps, but her DNA… her DNA had boundless questions for him. How could a mutant be born to a family of humans? David frequently boasted of his lineage, fully human as far back as he could trace. He had yet to decipher her existence. He had yet to be discouraged too.

He shoved her into the usual seat, at the very back of the room. A contraption designed to keep her perfectly still, so he could conduct any number of experiments and try to answer his questions. More often than not, however, he only uncovered more questions, so he was never truly sated. He kept her in that seat as long as he wanted, the restraint, a prod turned electric chair, paralysing her without the need for physical bounds.

The usual to begin with—with currents blasting between every fibre of her being, he took her blood, plucked a strand of her hair, swabbed the inside of her mouth.

Then onto the bigger stuff. Today's focus—her broken fingers. He picked at each one, bending them backwards against her will. She could not open her mouth to cry, emitting only a whimper in her throat.

"That is just noise," he mused dismissively, testing her forefinger. "Your kind do not feel pain."

He was wrong. Of course he was wrong. But there was no telling him that. Even without the paralysis, her jaw was locked with terror. "Mm. Where is your healing ability? I've seen mutants recover from disembowelment faster than this."

He wrenched back her ring finger. A scream hit her throat, jolting against her immovability, her agony trapped behind her teeth. Tears struck her cheeks and then so did his fist. "Just *noise*," he repeated, hissing. Spittle sprayed onto her; she flinched with a recoil she could not complete.

He moved away, pacing before the monitors. Images flashed, numbers and diagrams and animated predictions dancing across the screens in relentless jargon that he absorbed with ease. He nodded at something, moved to the centre tables. Metal scraped on metal, folders thumped as they were moved. Drawers raked on their sliders as they were snapped open, banging as they were slammed shut.

Whatever he was looking for evaded him for a few minutes. She could only watch, white-hot pins and needles scurrying up her arms, hand throbbing in time to her heartbeat.

He was talking – aloud or to her was never clear – "I'm beginning to wonder if there is a fault somewhere in your genes. A mutant's recovery is easily thrice as fast a human's, at the very least. But you, you have not got that component." He wrenched open another drawer, laughing with triumph as he finally located his prize.

A hammer. Just a regular hammer, like one to bang a nail into a wall or build a unit or… or smash her knee to splinters. Fire erupted up and down her leg; she screamed again, mouth sealed beyond her control. He gave a little *'heh'* of bemusement, already contemplating his next move. "Maybe you've not unlocked your healing ability yet." The hammer came down on her forearm. She heard the bone snap, sick rising on another scream, sitting on her tongue.

David smiled, flipping the tool in his hand. The clawed side disappeared into her shoulder, splurging a sticky warmth on her shirt. Dark spots swirled across her vision; she saw her blood drip from the hammer, over his fingers. "Mm," he said, leaning forward to examine the wound, "still nothing."

He straightened, flicking claret blood from the instrument. "No matter. Maybe it just needs a reason to come out."

Chapter Three

"Wow, you look terrible."

"Half of my face feels like it's on fire," Ashton deadpanned.

Killian winced, part-apologetic, part-sympathetic. Ashton frowned at him, eyes bloodshot and shadowed.

"I hope Dad's mates catch the gits that did it." Killian teetered on his toes, leaning close for a split second and wincing again. "In the meantime, I recommend a paper bag—"

"I recommend shushing."

"Denied." Killian flashed a lopsided grin. "Last one to breakfast smells like a rotten egg!"

He dashed off, clattering down the stairs. Ashton sighed. Rose's bedroom door swung open to his right.

"I'll kill him," she vowed, glowering fiercely, green face mask still on, hair in a towel. "Don't look at me like that," she defied, "if I don't kill him, you will."

"Aww, big sister affection."

"Mmph." She turned her nose up and retreated, slamming the door.

Ashton shook his head, the movement stabbing at the bruised side of his face. He was quiet on the stairs, stopping halfway, listening. As if on cue, David's laugh swam out from the kitchen.

Ashton backtracked, shutting the door to his bedroom. He sank down onto his bed, sighing. He would have to wait.

His eyes drifted around his room, a decent enough size, with matching furniture. He touched his cheek without thinking, eyes stinging. He hated this room. He never would have set it out so orderly, so spartan, so colourless. This was his father's decision. Ashton was to be his successor – also a paternal ideal – so he *had* to be like him. And to do that, he was heaped with workloads and expectations and sciences and threats… he had no choice.

He remembered the first one. The day his father caught a mutant for the first time.

"Fire manipulation," David bragged, brandishing his bandaged forearm like a trophy. "Tricky bugger. Didn't go down without a fight."

Ashton, then a few days shy of twelve, had innocently asked what was going to happen to the mutant.

"Are you going to help them, Dad?"

"Help them?" David demanded.

Ashton stepped back, tucking his hands to his side. His father half-turned, leaning towards him, the wooden chair he sat on creaking at the shift in weight. Ashton could still hear it now. David fixed those grey eyes on him, set his elbows on his knees, shoulders squared. When he spoke, his voice was a low growl. "It is a creature beyond help. I will study it. Test its limits. I will *break* the freak and all its kind. I do not *help* mutants," he sneered. "I'd better not hear you speak like that again. Is that clear?"

Ashton nodded, mouth dry.

About seven months later, the twins were born; grisly, chubby babies bundled in matching blankets. One had blonde hair, so fine it was hardly visible. The other, to Ashton's delight, had ginger fuzz. Two healthy baby girls, the perfect end to the Yachtman brood.

Violet was almost two when they first saw her powers.

They had been playing in the garden. Violet and Daisy were running as fast as their little legs could carry them, eager to keep up with their big siblings, giggling and stumbling as toddlers do.

Ashton passed the football to Marv, who passed it to Rose, who passed it to Killian. Overenthusiastic as always, Killian booted the ball as hard as he could. It flew for Daisy. It would have knocked her clean off her feet and, as a leather ball, it would have done untold damage to her little face, maybe worse.

"Ah!" Violet yelled, waving her hand.

The ball ricocheted off thin air, an impossible right angle at an incline, straight into the neighbour's garden.

Daisy was unhurt, watching a ladybird fly past her face, blissfully unaware. Violet had smiled at them, proud of her accomplishment. Rose had screamed for their father and Violet didn't smile again.

It had all gone downhill from there. Violet was never allowed to play with them, not any more. She was never allowed to do *anything*, shut in her room, shut in the house. Avoid windows and doors. Say nothing. Do nothing. Be nothing.

Ashton blinked, wiping carefully at his face and sniffing. He heard Rose's door open and close, always the last to go downstairs after her skin, hair, clothes, make-up routine. He rose, keeping his weight on the sides of his feet. He crept across the room, testing each spot before stepping. He cracked the door open just as cautiously, peering out onto the empty landing. There was chatter from downstairs, the clink of plates, the smell of pancakes. His stomach growled, but he could not think of food right now.

He sneaked across the landing, gently tapping his knuckles on Violet's door. She would hear him. She could hear a bird's wings beat at the end of the street. She would hear his taps.

A few seconds passed. David laughed, Killian childishly protesting something. Ashton tapped again.

"Vi," he breathed, "Vi, you OK?"

He waited twenty-eight seconds. He counted. Then he picked the lock. "Vi?" He stuck his head in, her room as dark and as dismal as ever. "Vi?"

She was on her mattress, on her side. He took a step in, closing the door with hardly a click. Her back was to him. Another step and he crouched at her side, touching her shoulder.

His hand brushed something crusted into her shirt, something still drying. He turned his hand over, seeing it shake as a coppery tang filled his nose. His fingers were stained red-brown with her blood.

Sand burned on his tongue, clogged his throat. "V-Vi…" he croaked. "Vi, wake up." With his clean hand, he moved her hair back from her face, leaning over her.

Her breath tickled his cheek, just. Faint, barely there. As he looked her over, heart thumping like a jackhammer behind his ribs, he saw that her arm and leg did not look right.

Her broken hand was in a far worse state than last night. Burns criss-crossed her skin, thin tendrils like tiny bolts of lightning on her arms, creeping up from below her neckline, splaying over her jaw and around her eyes.

He swallowed vomit. He hardly heard his own voice, so

frantic was his heart in his ears. "What did he do to you?"

"What are you doing?"

Ashton whirled around at the question, falling back and keeping Violet behind him.

David raised an eyebrow. He had come in unheard and unnoticed. "How did you get in here?"

"Door," Ashton replied brilliantly.

David sighed, lowering his head for a silent count of five.

"You've become increasingly disappointing each day," he said. He almost sounded sad about it too. Almost.

David smiled, a smile that only really lifted one corner of his mouth. "I'm not *overly* disappointed, mind you. I wasn't expecting much from you anyway." He shrugged a shoulder. "Rose has a better stomach for my work. She hasn't let me down."

"What did you do to Vi?"

"I was encouraging growth."

"You – you – look at what you did!" Ashton raged, now on his feet, fists clenched. "She could *die*! She could – she..." David took a step forward.

Ashton realised he was crying, hurriedly and futilely wiping at his face, irritating the bruise and splashing dark splodges of tears across half his vision. He held his ground, sniffing. "Help her."

"Heh." David snorted. "I've done what I can for it, but—
"

"You've done what you can for *you*," Ashton corrected, trembling. "*Help. Her,*" he ordered, dashing his sleeve over his cheek again.

His father began to laugh, shaking his head. "Help her," Ash persisted, "or I'll tell. I'll tell... I'll tell *everyone* about

33

her."

"No one would believe you."

"Someone will listen." Ashton defied, tipping his chin up. "And then what? What would that do to your precious *career*?"

David was solemn now, lips pursed in thought. He cricked his neck, attention wandering around the room.

For a whole three seconds, Ashton thought he had him, actually *had him*. He entertained the notion of Violet getting better, of them heading out that front door with whatever essentials they could filch, and never looking back. Warmth began to nibble at the edges of the dread stabbing away in his chest—he had done it.

But David Yachtman was not so easily bested.

He lunged, quicker than a heartbeat. Ashton slammed into the wall, head cracking on the drab construct, his father's hand crushing his windpipe.

"You love that *thing* so much," he snarled, spit spraying on Ashton's cheek, "then you can die with it."

Ashton clawed at the back of his father's hand; digging his fingers in, he grabbed his wrist as tightly as he could. He let his weight fall on the joint, back sliding down the wall, letting gravity take him. David grunted, bringing up his other hand. Ashton caught the fist on his forearm, the hand on his throat slipping a fraction. It was like breathing through a straw, but it was a start.

He brought his knee up, hard, catching David exactly where every man dreaded. Ashton gave a great shove. David toppled over, curling up on the floor as predicted.

Ashton wasted no time, scooping up his sister, cradling her to his chest. Her head lolled listlessly on his shoulder, chin dipping.

David made a grab for him as he stepped over. Ashton spun awkwardly, avoiding capture, and somehow staying upright, although he did crash into the door. He crouched slightly, fingers slipping on the handle at first, but then he got it. He was out, David cursing behind him.

"What's all that—?" Rose appeared at the bottom of the stairs, freezing, when Ashton hurried down, Violet's bloodied, unconscious form in his arms. "What—?"

"Stop him!" David shouted, pulling himself up on the banister.

Killian and Marv were hanging out of the living-room doorway. Daisy stuck her head out of the kitchen, puzzled. "Stop him!"

No one moved. They took one look at Violet and stilled. Ashton was out the front door without resistance.

It swung shut behind him, he heard it thump closed. Did not look back; there was nothing he wanted to see one last time.

"We did it, Vi," he breathed, hurrying across the street.

It was still early, hardly anyone out, most curtains still drawn. He rounded the corner, over the road again and down an alley that would take him to the backroads.

Violet groaned, paler than he had ever known. "Stay with me," he pleaded, not daring to speak above a whisper, "we're on our way, just stay with me."

Chapter Four

"Miiiiiichaaeel!"

"Fiiiiiinn!"

"Good news!"

"You've decided to put a bag over your head?" Michael smirked. Finn huffed at him, tucking his tablet to his chest.

"I'll put a bag over *your* head, you keep up with that attitude," he grumbled.

Michael gave an innocent smile, setting down his book. He rested his elbows on his desk, chin on his laced fingers. Finn eyed him sidelong.

"Are you going to tell me?" Michael asked.

"Are you going to listen?" Finn countered.

"I'm rather busy."

"Pfft. You'd have free time if you stopped reading for two seconds."

"Blasphemy."

"OK, fine. Be like that then. I won't tell you that Brenda called to tell me – *me*, not you – that it finally happened, and I won't tell you that Brenda told me – again, *me*, not you—"

"I get the idea."

"—that Yachtman got a whack in his..." Finn gestured down, repeating the motion Ashton had taken to cause the said whack. "Doesn't matter how high and mighty you are—a wallop to your jewels will render any bloke helpless."

"Wish I'd seen it."

"Yeah, me too." Finn sighed wistfully. "Anyway, the kid's

36

gone AWOL and he took the mutant with him." His smile wilted, fanning the tablet and tapping it on the palm of his hand. "Brenda says she's real hurt."

"We need to find them. Send scouts and—"

"Comb the area? Way ahead of you, Mike." Finn hopped up on the desk, crossing his feet at the ankles and began typing on his tablet. "Got three teams already on the move, and I sent Brenda to peer in Yachtman's windows."

"Um, *why*?"

"'Cos she can turn invisible and spy on people."

"You've got her waiting to see if Yachtman gets another whack, haven't you?"

"It's for scientific purposes."

"I'm sure it is." Michael nodded solemnly.

Finn huffed, rolling his eyes.

"Thought you were supposed to be smart."

"I will fire you."

"Nah. The nepotism is strong with this one." Finn poked him in the head, grinning. Michael swatted his hand away, gaining a slight crease to his brow. "Ooh, you've got that look. What is it?"

"Not now."

"Why?"

"Because it could be really, really good," Michael began carefully, "or... it could kill us all."

"Wow. Optimism much." Finn sighed. He was quiet for a moment, thoughts flitting over his face. "Wait... how did you come up with that? What do you know? No, don't start reading again, I'm talking to you!"

Michael calmly turned his page.

Finn glowered. "I hate you."

"I'm aware."

"Really hate you."

"Oh, stop. You're breaking my heart."

"Brenda's my new best friend now."

"Good for you."

Chapter Five

No coat. No shoes. No supplies. Nowhere to go. Ashton had had to divert away from the residential area, targeting one of the many frosted fields on the outskirts of town. Woods covered the upper side of the field, their leafless boughs clattering softly in a winter breeze. This is where they hid now.

He had used his hoodie to staunch and bandage Violet's bleeding shoulder. He wasn't a doctor of any degree, but it was all he could do. As for her broken hand, arm and leg… he tried not to move her too much. She lay beside him, on her back, breathing fitfully. He sat as close to her as he dared, fearful of causing more pain, but also scared of the cold biting into his skin and sinking deeper. They had taken up shelter under a massive oak tree. Mud soaked into his socks and lower legs. Suppressing a shiver, he looked back over at his sister. He could not allow himself to think on it, but the question remained—how much longer would she last? Blood had saturated her shirt long before he wrapped the wound, now dry. Splotches of blood had stopped growing on his hoodie, but he did not think for a second that it was because he had successfully stopped the bleeding.

"This wasn't the plan, Vi," he mumbled, sitting back against the trunk. His shoulders and spine wailed at the movement, having been caught carrying her all morning and not liking the change. He stretched his legs out, feet feeling like had walked miles on hot knives.

A sigh escaped him without him realising it, eyes burning. He looked over at her again, the motion firing up the new bruises on his neck. They had escaped. But at what cost?

He sniffed, gingerly wiping at his eyes with trembling fingers.

A twig snapped. There was a *thump*, someone swore. Someone else laughed. Ashton rose to a crouch, turning to Violet, ready to lift and run.

David had a mutant-tracking army at his disposal. If push came to shove, Ashton would have only a branch in defence.

"... lost, aren't we?" The voice came from somewhere to his right.

"Probably. Poxy Finn. Bet he's getting a real kick out of this."

There was the sound of a hand smacking something plastic, another curse. "I swear he always gives me the dodge gear."

"Let me try."

"No, it's mine."

"Do you *want* to go home today?"

A moment's pause.

"Ugh, fine."

"Thank you."

"I want it back though."

"What are you, five?"

"Five stars, yeah."

"Mmm, maybe a five on a scale of one to ten. In the right light."

"I don't have to be nice to you."

"You're nice to me?"

"Oh, shut up."

Ashton peered around the tree. Their footsteps had stopped. He could see them, two men with their backs to him. They stood fifteen, maybe twenty feet away, huddled together to examine a tablet of sorts.

The one on the left was brown skinned with his hair in neat cornrows. The other was white with messy, blue-dyed hair. They wore matching red parkas, black cargo trousers and sturdy black boots.

He ducked back, racking his brain. As far as he could remember, his father had never mentioned a Finn before. Although, his organisation was large, with many departments. There would be a Finn there somewhere, no doubt about it.

They had to move.

He was slow and cautious in picking Violet up again, holding his breath as he did so.

The movement hurt her. She groaned, grimacing as she turned her head into his shoulder.

"What was that?" The blue-haired one asked. Ashton held perfectly still.

"You heard it too?"

"No, I often ask, 'what was that' without a reason."

"Really?"

"You're not good with sarcasm, are you?" Cornrows didn't answer. Ashton risked another peek. Blue Hair gestured to his friend, tapping his ear and circling a finger around their surroundings. Cornrows just stared at him. "Oh Seltik, help me." Blue Hair grumbled. "I said, keep an ear out and look around."

"Oh. Why can't you just use words?"

"Um, stealth? You know what stealth is, right?"

"With your track record, I should be asking you that."

"Just look. Finn said the kid was hurt. We have to find her." Blue Hair turned.

Ashton hid again. His heart was banging away behind his ribs, determined to break out. He heard them move, footsteps getting closer. "I saw you," Blue Hair called, "there's no point hiding from us, mate."

"No, see, that sounds threatening. Let me talk to him." Blue Hair blew a raspberry, but let Cornrows take over. "We just want to help, mate. I'm Kurtis. This is Paul. You're Yachtman's boy, ain't you?"

Ashton bit the inside of his cheek, ducking his head, holding Violet closer. "We know you ran away. And we know your sister's hurt. We've got people who can help her. And you."

Ashton squeezed his eyes shut, tears falling onto his cheeks, splashing on Violet's hair.

"Probably should tell him we're mutants."

"We can do that?"

"You've literally told him everything else." Blue Hair huffed, possibly rolling his eyes.

"Oh, yeah. Uh, well, in that case, we're mutants. We can help."

"Full offence, your dad sucks."

"Heard you got him right where it hurts though."

"Least he deserves."

"I wanted to see it."

"Same."

"Are you going to come out? It's meant to rain this afternoon and Paul did his hair this morning. You do *not* want to ruin Paul's hair."

"No, you most certainly do not," Paul agreed.

Ashton didn't move.

Paul swore under his breath. "This is taking forever."

There was a snap, Paul clicking his fingers. The tree Ashton was using as cover shivered. Its roots groaned, rising, and shifting, pushing against his back. He darted away, spun around. The oak tree *walked* on its many roots, slithering, and stomping six feet to the left. It reminded him of a video he had seen once, of an octopus moving on the sand.

The tree stopped, branches jolting, and replanted itself, roots sinking into the earth. If he didn't know better, it could have been there for years.

Paul grinned at him. "Now, tell me if one of you dumb-dumb humans can do that?"

***

Ashton relented. To save Violet, he had to. Paul and Kurtis appreciated his cooperation, standing on either side of him. Kurtis held his arm; Paul gripped his shoulder.

"Oh, forewarning. Porting can make you a bit sick the first few times."

"Porting?" Ashton echoed. Kurtis nodded.

In the blink of an eye, the woods vanished. Shadows swirled around them, ten tonnes of motion sickness sucker-punched him, and then it was over. "Ugh." He groaned, sinking to his knees. He managed to hold onto Violet, heaving.

"No, no, no, don't you *dare* throw up." That was a new voice.

Looking up brought bile up to his mouth. "I mean it!" the man said. "One bit of sick and I'm turfing you out."

He was similar in age to Ashton, maybe a little shorter.

Light-brown skin, black, choppy hair, and olive-green eyes that frowned at the sickly newcomer. He wore jeans and a navy-blue T-shirt with block-white letters on that read, *GIVE ME YOUR MONEY.*

He poked Ashton on the forehead. A sweet coolness bristled through him, chasing away the nausea. "Right, learn this and learn this quickly—I do *not* do sick, and I do *not* do babies. Or eyes." He blinked, lowered his hand, and looked down at Violet. "Give," he ordered, holding his hands out. Ashton did no such thing. The man glowered. "Giiiiiiive," he repeated, drawing the word out slowly and pointedly.

"Uh, mate…" Paul helped Ashton to his feet. "This is Finn. He's our chief medic."

"Better do as he says," Kurtis warned, eyes widening as he nodded seriously. "I didn't and I found a bloody femur in my bed." He dropped his voice to a terrified whisper. "I don't know where he got it."

"I told you a hundred times, I *borrowed* it." Finn huffed. "Last chance, mate. Give." He made grabby motions. Paul and Kurtis nodded in encouragement. Ashton passed Violet over. Finn smirked, vanishing, and reappearing further down the room, where he laid her on a bed.

There were dozens of beds, the room easily as long as a football pitch, but quite narrow. Each bed's headboard was pushed up against the walls, left and right, with four feet between them. The walls were a soft yellow colour; the lights were gentle and shone kindly off metal cabinets and cupboards that were stationed between the beds and against the back wall. The floor was lino, white and pastel-blue tiles, the blue matching that of the bedding and the curtains open in front of long windows just below the ceiling.

Finn was poking at Violet, mumbling to himself, rubbing his jaw. "Kathy!" he called without looking up. "Kathy!"

"What?" a woman demanded, sticking her head out from a door Ashton couldn't see, one hidden just past a large medicine cabinet. "I am doing *your* paperwork, *again*. What do you want?"

"There's a human over there. Patch him up for me, will you? And make sure he's not sick." Finn waved in the general direction of the newcomers.

Kathy turned to face them, frowning. Her hair had been dyed blonde, brunette growing out at the roots. She came into the main room in a white T-shirt and knee-length red skirt. She was older than Finn, forty-something, about shoulder-height to Ashton, wide at the hips, and rather matronly.

"Why is there a human here? Does Michael know?"

"Special permission," Finn said, shining a light in Violet's eyes.

"Mmph," Kathy said. As she approached, she cut a steely blue-eyed glance at Paul and Kurtis. Both stood straight, hurrying to make themselves presentable. She held her hand out and Kurtis returned the tablet they had been arguing over. "How did *you two* find them?"

"Don't know." Kurtis shrugged.

"Got lost," Paul supplied at the same time.

They glared at each other challengingly until Kathy snapped her fingers. They started and looked at her, part-apologetic, part-guilty.

"Do you two need medical attention?"

"No, ma'am," they chorused.

"Then sod off and report to Michael."

"Yes, ma'am." They vanished into thin air. Ashton

45

blinked, head spinning.

"What's your name?" Kathy had to tap his uninjured cheek to get his attention. "Name," she demanded.

"A-Ashton."

"Well, A-Ashton. I heard you got Yachtman good." She smiled slyly. "You'll fit in well here."

"Aha!" Finn declared, clapping sharply. Ashton started forward. Kathy grabbed his arm with a strength that surprised him, steering him back into place.

"He may look like an idiot—"

"Heard that!"

"—but Finn knows what he's doing. Let's get you sorted out. You're tracking mud all over my floor."

It took Kathy a grand total of twenty-three seconds to fix him up. With a gentle touch of her fingertips, his bruises stopped hurting, then faded, then healed altogether. The swelling around his eye went down. She tapped a finger on his throat, telling him to hum. "Is that the Pokémon theme song?" she laughed. "I'd kill for a Chansey around here, you know? No, no talking, just hum." At his confusion, she smiled. "I'm listening for damage to your vocal cords. Yes, I can do that." Her smile turned smug. He smiled weakly in response, immediately ordered to hum again.

On the twenty-fourth second, she pulled him to his feet. "There's a shower room just through there. I'm saying this in the nicest way possible—use soap." She grimaced a smile. Ashton scrunched his nose and she laughed, slugging him in the arm good-naturedly. "Oops!" she said, as she knocked him back onto the bed. "Sorry! Temporarily forgot you were human!" She helped him up again, waving imaginary dust from his shoulder. "I'll get some clean clothes for you."

"Thank you." Ashton went off to shower – with the strongly advised, lemon-scented soap – and Kathy went off to find him something to wear.

"How is he?" Finn asked. He was still tending to Violet. Her arm and leg were neatly splinted, then he had cleaned and carefully stitched her shoulder. Electric burns covered in a pink salve, riddled, and webbed across her skin, venturing under clean, white cotton pyjamas, her old, bloodied clothes now sitting in the hazardous waste bin. One of her hands was trussed up in bandages stained with Finn's home remedy ointment, and he was now setting up IV lines and blood transfusions.

"He'll be fine. It's this one I'm worried about." Kathy took hold of Violet's wrist, counting her pulse.

Finn pursed his lips, checking the needles in his patient's arm. "What have you given her?"

"Now," he said haughtily, "if I told you all my secrets, I'd lose my mysterious allure." Kathy snorted, making him scowl. "You," he declared, cutting her a look, "are no longer on my Christmas card list."

"You *never* send out Christmas cards."

"But if I *did*... *yoooooouuuuu* wouldn't get one!"

"That hurts, Finn. That really hurts."

"Good. Suffer."

Chapter Six

"If you *have* to sleep here, could you *please* not snore?" Finn glowered at him. Ashton blinked, two seconds after Finn had rudely awoken him, trying to remember where he was.

Finn had kindly – read *bullied-by-Kathy* – agreed to let Ashton stay in the medbay, offering a bed next to Violet. She was yet to wake up, but Finn assured him – easily a dozen times an hour – that she would be as right as rain. "My medicine works better than anything you dumb-dumb humans can come up with."

Now, Finn was towering over him, a pillow clutched between his fists. Ashton stared blankly at him. The pillow was squeezed like an accordion. What might have been an attempt at a smile spread across Finn's face, although it looked more like he had sat on a porcupine. "Little bit of advice if you're staying here—*mutants* can hear *everything*. That includes your snoring."

"I don't—"

"Like a baby chainsaw," Finn continued, ignoring him, "with a chest infection. But it quickly became a ticking-clock noise."

"A what?"

"A ticking-clock noise," Finn repeated slowly, the agonising smile falling into a 'contemplating murder' deadpan. "If I hear a noise like a ticking clock or a dripping tap or a baby chainsaw snore, I can't *unhear* it and insomnia hits me." He cocked his head. "Assuming you are fond of your limbs being in their rightful places and not forcefully swapped around by an insomniac wielding a pillow, I take it you wouldn't mind rolling onto your *side* and killing that chainsaw before I do?" His mouth twitched, a second-long reappearance of that sat-on-a-spiky-animal smile. Ashton nodded, biting his lip.

"Y-yeah, sorry. I'll... I'll roll."

"Thank you." Finn turned away.

"Um, Finn?" Ashton sat up on his elbows. Finn drew to a stop, shoulders hunching.

"If you are having a medical emergency, I suggest you reschedule for the morning."

"No. I wanted to say thank you. For saving Vi. I... I don't know what I'd have done if I lost her."

"Probably fallen into a crippling depression where you lose all interest in self-care, hobbies and loved ones, form a harmful addiction that leaves you bankrupt and homeless and die a slow, painful death on a cold, lonely street with all your organs shutting down from substance abuse and hypothermia." Finn glanced over his shoulder, showing a dead-eyed smirk. "Best-case scenario anyway."

"You strike me as a real ray of sunshine."

"If I have to be a ray, I want to be a death ray. Now, good night. Save your dying woes for a more reasonable time and *sleep on your side.*"

***

Ashton awoke quite early – someone had been superglued to a chair after falling prey to a prank – so Finn, Kathy and another medic, Jeevan, were rushing to help.

After they stopped laughing.

"Um, excuse me." The chair victim, Sara, frowned at them all. She was sixteen, seventeen maybe, with short mouse-brown hair and pale-blue eyes. Her friend, who had set the prank – Lacey – was standing beside her, battling to keep a straight face, silent tears of laughter streaming down her cheeks.

Sara glared at the medics, tipping her nose up haughtily. "If you are *quite* finished—"

Finn snorted, Kathy wheezed and doubled over.

Sara tried lifting herself up, feet sliding on the lino floor. "Ow-ow-ow-ow-ow…"

"OK, OK." Jeevan motioned for her to still, wiping his eyes. He was a tall, sturdily built man, in his late twenties, with rich, brown skin and richer, browner eyes. He wore a black turban, beard neatly trimmed, a white button-up shirt with the sleeves folded up and black jeans. He allowed himself a few more giggles, gently pushing on Sara's shoulders to have her stop straining. "Right, let's just—Finn, control yourself. We'll have you off in a jiffy," he assured Sara. "Ignore my colleagues."

"Done." Sara nodded once.

Between Jeevan and Lacey, they carried Sara away, holding the legs of the chair. Sara squealed at them, grasping the seat, promising revenge should they drop her. Finn and Kathy trailed behind, still snickering.

"What was all that?" Ashton jolted at the voice, hope surging through his chest like a summery heat.

"Vi!" He leapt from his bed with a relieved laugh, crashing onto his sister. He squashed himself on the bed next to her, hugging her tightly. "Oh, thank God you're OK!"

"God?" Finn was back, raging and flapping his arms. "Don't thank *God*, thank me! *I* did all the work, not *God*! *They* didn't do *anything*!"

Kathy appeared, taking him by the arm. She smiled at the siblings, steering Finn away and nodding along to his grumblings.

"Oxygen," Violet requested, voice a tiny squeak muffled against his chest.

"Sorry!" He released her, cupping her face in his hands. She went cross-eyed to look at him, watching his gaze dart about her face, her hands, looking for any sign of an injury. "Are you hurt? Any pain? Do you want food?" He fussed over her for a good few minutes, not letting her get a word in edgeways, squishing her cheeks, hugging her, kissing her forehead and then blowing a raspberry on her cheek when she complained.

He had calmed a little, holding her gently, when Sara walked out, wearing white cotton pyjama bottoms, her ruined jeans slung over her arm. Lacey was three steps behind her, carrying the chair (now littered with bits of denim) and still laughing.

"Sara, I'm sorry!" she cackled, dark eyes brimming with mischief. "Sara!"

"I'm not talking to you!"

"Why don't we sit and talk about it?" Lacey suggested innocently.

"I will never sit again!" Sara fumed, wrenching the door open. Lacey leant on the chair, melting into giggles once more. Sara flung her a rude hand gesture, slamming the door behind her. After a moment to try to compose herself, Lacey went after

her. They could hear them all the way down the hall, one laughing, one yelling. The medics re-emerged, bemusement still flitting between them.

"Oh, look," Kathy smiled, smacking Finn on the arm and pointing, "she's proper awake."

"No thanks to God." Finn cut Ashton a look. He tried to shoo him away, fussing with the IV.

Ashton made to step aside, small fingers clinging to his shirt.

Violet didn't say anything, tears pooling at the corners of her eyes. She looked up at him, hands shaking.

"It's all right, Vi," Ashton promised, squeezing her wrists kindly. "They're like you. They helped us." She bit her bottom lip, glancing at the medics, ducking her head. "Trust me," he urged, "I'll be right here, OK?" She stared at something past his shoulder, clinging to his hands. He kissed the top of her head, smiling encouragingly. "We got out," he told her. "We did it."

"Ashton hit Yachtman in the diiiiii—" Finn drew out the noise, aware Kathy and Jeevan were side-eyeing him warningly, one on either side of him. "—iiii, soft spot." His eyes flicked from colleague to colleague, bumping his fist in his hand. "Saved it. Yes. Flawless." He nodded seriously.

"You hit him?" Violet asked quietly, looking up at her brother. He nodded. The rest of the story could wait.

"Anyway, I'm Finn. This is Kathy and Jeevan. You already know Ashton, I hope."

"Finn likes to think he's funny."

"I'm hilarious."

"No, no." Kathy poked him in the elbow. "Humorous."

"Oh. *Oh*. That was *terrible*."

"Now you know how we feel."

"I have a patient," Finn turned his nose up at them both, "be gone, underlings."

They both smacked him, a whack to each shoulder, then wandered off, mimicking him quite deftly. "As I said, I am Finn. *I* saved you, even if this idiot," he jabbed a thumb at Ashton, "thanked *God* for it."

"Would it help if I apologised?"

"No." Finn shooed him away again, checking the needle in Violet's arm. He shone a tiny light in her eyes, told her to stick her tongue out so he could check her throat, wriggle her fingers and toes, and then finally, asked her to hum the Muppets song.

"What was that for?" Ashton asked once she stopped humming. Finn smirked.

"I like the Muppets."

"I like Fozzie Bear," Violet mumbled, fiddling with the hem of her shirt. Finn patted her head, smirk softening into a more amiable smile.

"Well, nothing's broken any more. Bloods are normal, reactions are normal—" He jabbed her in the knee to make sure, nodding at the jolt that responded. "—and I'd say you're all tickety-boo." He wriggled his fingers, reaching behind her ear. A lollipop sprung from nowhere, presented to her with an "Oh me, where did *that* come from?"

"Green!" Violet recognised. She reached up to take it, freezing with her fingers around the sweet, not touching it. She hesitated, withdrawing her hand. Her head tipped in Ashton's direction, clutching his shirt again.

"Mm." Finn rubbed his jaw. "My lollipops are never rejected." He narrowed his eyes at her in thought. "OK,

53

counterpoint." He rolled the sweet between his thumb and forefinger and then he held two. "Is that better? If you don't like green," he shook the sticks, "I have red. Orange. Purple. Blue. Cream. Pink. Pink *and* cream." With each colour, he shook the lollipops, the flavour changing before their eyes in seamless flows of all the colours of the rainbow.

He returned them to green, summoning a third when she still didn't take them. "I am baffled," he admitted. Ashton leant down, an arm around her shoulders.

"You can have them if you want. You're free now."

"I can do all the colours if you want." Finn cupped his hands, tipping a cascade of multicoloured lollipops into her lap. Violet stared at them, wide-eyed, hand hovering over the pile uncertainly. "Mm. Don't tell Kathy. And make sure you brush your teeth. Sugar rots your teeth, you know." He fashioned a lollipop for himself, red and without the wrapper, sucking on it thoughtfully.

He noticed Violet was watching him and wriggled the stick between his teeth.

"What do you say?" Ashton prompted.

"Thank you," Violet said, barely audible. Finn smiled around his sweet, patting her head again.

"Seriously, don't tell Kathy though. She'll make me put a pound in the Sugar Jar again. Like a swear jar, but for handing out sweets." He explained at Ashton's look. He made a face at Violet's stash. "May need a bigger jar."

***

Finn approached them again just after lunch. Ashton had made Violet laugh by using carrot sticks as fangs. He spat them out when he noticed the medic watching him.

"Yeah, anyway…" Finn looked at Violet. "Michael wants to see you." She stared at him blankly and he gave a little start. "Oh, right. Michael is, uh… he's big boss. Owns the place, runs the place, brains of the place. Does lots of place things." He scratched at his chin. "So, yeah, when you're ready."

Violet looked from him to Ashton, pointing a finger at the latter in silent question. "Yeah, he comes too. He's, like, your guardian or whatever? I dunno." He shrugged.

Finn clapped once, holding his hands out, palms up, to catch a pile of clothing. "I won't drag you out in your pyjamas," he promised, setting the pile on Violet's shins. "Just be ready in five minutes."

Four minutes later – Finn grew bored and fidgety – they were climbing the stairs. Wherever they were, it was busy and lively, stocked chocker with mutants. Violet clung to Ashton's arm as they followed Finn, keeping her head down, watching the floor pass beneath her feet. Ashton kept her close but spent most of the walk trying to absorb every detail.

He saw mutants of all ages and shapes and sizes and *species*—a woman in her late fifties walked by with red monarch butterfly wings folded against her back. She was wolfing down a pasty. Finn greeted her with a fist bump, neither of them breaking their stride.

There were families, children playing and racing around the adults, squealing when they were caught or when they saw a friend. There were couples here and there, holding hands, sitting on the floor in the hallways for lunch and causing a general nuisance, but it seemed people here had grown accustomed to hopping over them. Mutants that appeared from nowhere, mutants that vanished into nowhere. Mutants juggling fireballs or electrifying their friends to make their hair stand on end or making children float to play on the ceiling.

Finn noticed Ashton staring slack-jawed at someone with elephant ears.

"Some mutants take on animal characteristics. Sometimes, although quite rare now, they'll be a humanoid version of the animal. We used to have a woman who was a lizard." He sighed, shoulders slumping.

"What happened?" Ashton asked kindly.

"She moved to New York to play up that lizard-people-in-the-sewer thing."

"Oh." Ashton said, having expected something a bit more… dead?

Finn nodded earnestly, as if Ashton had said something profound.

"I know right? Bloody cheek going without me!"

"You're… not a lizard?"

"I could be."

"How?"

"I'm still working on that."

"What?"

"Mate, mutant genetics are *teeming* with possibilities." Ashton stared at him. "Bah." Finn waved away all unasked questions. Ashton decided that was probably the best thing, and he turned to his sister.

"You OK, Vi?" he asked, touching her cheek to get her attention.

"Lots of stairs," she puffed.

"Only three more flights to go!" Finn said cheerily, brandishing a finger in the air.

"Um, if you guys can teleport—" Ashton began.

"Just port."

"— why are we walking up eight flights of stairs?"

"Mm, I ask myself that too." Finn sulked. "One, I need to see how her ladyship here is walking on that leg—remarkably well, may I say. Here, have a lolly." He plucked a green one from the air. Violet took it with a quiet smile of thanks, tucking the wrapper into Ashton's pocket. "And two," Finn sighed, rubbing wearily at his face, "Michael wants to finish his chapter. Trust me, you do *not* want to stop him finishing his chapter."

"He reads?"

"Incessantly." Finn grumbled. He hopped up the last few steps, landing neatly on the next floor. He stretched his arms over his head, looking around. "Mmph." He wrinkled his nose. "Floor Six. I hate Floor Six."

"Floor Six hates you too, Finn." Someone walking past said, not even looking up from their book. Finn mimicked them in a higher pitch, *blah-blah-blah-ing* with his hand. The other mutant snapped their fingers. Finn sighed, looking down.

His jeans and T-shirt had been replaced with a giant, boss-eyed, head-to-toe moss-green frog costume. He looked at his hands, encased in gloves with long, webbed fingers, said gloves seamless with the sleeves, and sighed again.

"Floor Six." He spread his arms, trying for a *ta-da* smile only for the top half on the large headpiece to fall, the mouth closing. "I hate Floor Six," his muffled voice protested. "This way." He gestured with a flipper and began to walk again.

Except, now with large, webbed shoes to match his new large, webbed gloves, he walked like a dog trying shoes on for the first time, hitching his knees up, feet slapping on the floor. Ashton spluttered, laughter bubbling up. Violet, surprising herself with a giggle next to him, broke his resolve. Finn pretended not to hear their amusement, especially when it came to yet more stairs. "Floor Six," he explained somewhere before Floor Eight, "is full of tricksters. All the inconvenience to mild chaotic types go there." He pushed the mouth open, inhaling cooler air.

"Inconvenience?" Ash repeated. "Mild chaotic? What?"

"Mmm, basically their powers are to upset order. Like magical pranksters. They know I hate frogs, so I am," he gestured at himself, spreading his arms, "like this."

"Why though?" Ashton laughed. "What did you do?"

"Nothing!" Finn insisted.

The siblings exchanged sceptical looks and he sighed. "Long story short, there were five chickens, a very large spoon and a Mercedes with three wheels. And a stick." He nodded seriously, as if that last item was the most dreaded of them all. "They haven't forgiven me yet, so… frog."

Violet took the lolly out of her mouth, pointing at him with it.

"Why do you hate frogs?" she asked.

"Also, a long story." Finn shuddered. They reached the top.

Ashton heaved a sigh of relief, convinced his legs were planning to walk out on him. Or perhaps, just collapse into exhausted piles of goop.

Finn led them on a little bit more, stopping outside a pastel orange door. He knocked once, followed by two quick knocks and then a big *thump*.

"It's open!" someone called from inside.

The room was bigger than expected, maybe the size of a large dining room. Bookshelves lined every wall, floor to ceiling, artfully built around windows that looked out onto a grey winter's afternoon. There were desks of varying styles scattered higgledy-piggledy around the room, laden with yet more books and paper and pen pots.

Beanbags piled in the back left corner in a range of bright colours. A fireplace on the right-hand wall, filled with brilliant pink flames, mismatched armchairs arranged before it. The floor was just as bizarre: dark wood lost under dozens of rugs and mats. There was one large, dark redwood desk in the middle of the room, as smothered with books and papers as its comrades. A black, well-worn leather swivel chair sat behind it, in which sat a man.

He was about Ashton's age, give or take a year or two, his skin tone just a tad darker than Finn's. His hair was either a very, very dark-brown or black, Ashton couldn't tell, but his eyes were a rich earthy brown that sparkled with amber hues in the firelight. He wore glasses, black, rounded frames that sat a little crooked across his nose. There was a splodge of blue ink on his cheek, perhaps he hadn't noticed. A white T-shirt with a penguin holding a sign that yelled 'SAVE US!', also stained with ink.

The man smiled at them as they approached, grinning at Finn the Frog like all his Christmases had come at once. "Floor Six?"

"Floor Six," the medic confirmed miserably.

"Suits you."

"Knew you'd say that."

The man pushed away from his desk, rising and moving around it. He wore black jeans, folded paper sticking out of his back pocket.

"I'm Michael." He smiled, offering Ashton his hand.

Ashton shook it, a tingle wriggling up to his elbow.

"I'm…" He faltered, distracted by those amber flecks in Michael's eyes. It wasn't a trick of the firelight—that colouration was real, not amber, but a soft pink up close, dashed through the brown like reckless paint splatters.

"Ashton?" Michael guessed politely.

Heat crept into Ashton's face, realising he had left that sentence unfinished remarkably longer than acceptable, just to gawk at this man's eyes.

Michael shook his hand and let go. The tingle faded away. "And you must be Violet." He crouched in front of her, smiling warmly. She squashed herself to Ashton's side, hiding behind his arm. "I see Finn's been piling you with sweets. Has he been looking after you?" From somewhere in the frog, Finn spluttered, offended. Michael ignored him, patiently waiting for Violet's answer.

She gave a small nod and his smile widened. Ashton bit the inside of his cheek, resolutely deciding to watch Finn try and shake off a webbed glove.

He looked around when Violet swayed, gripping her elbow. She was looking at the floor again, eyes shifting between two rugs. Michael tipped his head curiously, raising an eyebrow. Violet looked at him, biting her thumbnail, and then up at Ashton. She said nothing, brow creasing.

"What?" he asked. She shook her head and looked down again.

"I wanted to talk to you about what we do here," Michael said, standing. "Is that OK?"

Violet nodded again, and he gestured widely, welcoming them to the room. "Would you like to sit by the fire or flop on the beanbags?"

"Flop?" she repeated. Michael laughed. Behind him, Finn the Frog aimed for the beanbags at a dead sprint, knees high, frog shoes flopping, launching himself onto the mass and promptly vanishing, except for his webbed feet.

"Stuck," he announced. When there was no immediate rescue, he sighed, feet crossing at the ankles. "If this is how I die, I welcome it."

"You'll get used to Finn," Michael assured them. "Where would you like to go?"

"Beanbags please," Violet requested quietly.

Michael gave a flourish of his hand.

"Ladies first."

Violet picked a green one, sinking into it and nearly disappearing like Finn. Ashton had better luck on a blue one. Michael swatted Finn's feet aside and dropped onto an orange one.

"You OK over there?" he asked, as Violet kicked and squirmed. She managed to scoot into a more upright position, holding still lest the beanbag ate her.

Michael shifted to retrieve the wad of paper from his back pocket, tapping it on his thigh twice before unfolding it. He held out a hand, a pen flying in from one of the many pen pots. Violet stared at him, flexing her fingers.

"Left." She noticed.

"Yes, I am left." Michael wriggled the pen in a wave. "All mutants are left-handed."

"Why?"

"Devil spawn," Finn supplied, pulling himself up and slumping sideways, lying beside Michael and elbowing him. Michael simply closed the frog's mouth. "Knew you'd do that."

"Mutants are just left-handed. Uh, that does not mean all lefties are mutants, but all mutants are lefties." Violet looked at her hand. Ashton bit his lip. It was the hand their father had broken.

Michael scribbled his pen on the paper, testing it. "Have you seen much of the place?"

Violet looked at Ashton.

"No," he replied. "The hospital—"

"Medbay." Finn's muffled voice corrected.

"—and stairs. Lots of stairs."

"It's good cardio," Finn interjected, prying the frog's mouth open. "Help me out here, Mike. I'm boiling."

"You know my terms," Michael responded calmly, drawing something on his paper.

Finn huffed, waving his hand. Appearing beside the pen in Michael's hand, an orange lollipop. "Thank you." He snapped the fingers of his right hand. Finn was suddenly back in his normal clothes.

"Oh, thank Seltik." He heaved a sigh of relief, star fishing on his beanbag. "Thanks, mate."

"Stay away from Floor Six."

"No promises."

"What's Seltik?" Ashton butted in. "I heard, um... the bloke with the blue hair?"

"Paul."

"Paul said something about Seltik when he and the other—"

"Kurtis."

"Yes, Kurtis. When they found us."

"Seltik is basically... mm..." Michael tapped his pen. "You'd best understand it as Seltik being our god, but it's not a religion. If the stories are anything to go by, Seltik was believed to be the first mutant."

"How was he—? Uh, she—?"

"They," Michael supplied. "Created?" Ashton nodded. "Don't know," Michael shifted a shoulder. "No one knows." He circled his pen at Violet. "I could ask the same about you." She stayed quiet, looking down at her lap. "Not to worry. I do like a challenge. Otherwise, I wouldn't have put up with Finn for this long."

"Ditto."

"Um," Ashton raised his hand, "next question. How did Paul and Kurtis find us? Like, how did they know—why were they—? Why were you looking for us?" Again, Michael aimed his pen at Violet.

"Don't think for a second that Yachtman can keep secrets from us." His smile turned devious, as he glanced sidelong at Finn. Ashton looked from one to the other.

"What, you guys bugged our house?"

"Pfft, no. That's too easy." Finn snickered. He rubbed his hands together gleefully. "You know Brenda, right?"

"Brenda-next-door?" The pair nodded, still grinning at their inside joke. "What about Brenda-next-door?"

"She's a mutant," Michael replied simply.

Ashton snorted in disbelief. Violet stared. Michael visibly held back a smile. "Actually..." he scribbled something down. "All of your neighbours are mutants."

"Come again?"

"Tell him the best bit." Finn hissed, giggling behind his fingers. Michael motioned to him—*in a second*.

"All of them—?"

"Are mutants, yes. There's, what, a dozen or so houses on

your street? Yachtman has been to every single one, hasn't he? Barbeques, fireworks, Christmas, Chinese New Year, the works. He was there, wasn't he? You and your siblings too."

"Then why did no one step in?" Ashton demanded, squeezing his hands under his arms. "Where were all these mutants when he had her beaten near to death? Where were they when he was more than happy to let her starve in a glorified airing cupboard? Where *were* they when he told *all of us* to pretend that she didn't exist? Even her own *twin* forgets her."

"Did you ever look under the stairs?" The question threw Ashton, his temper rolling up in confusion. He glared at Michael, but Michael was writing down something else, eventually looking up like he didn't even notice Ashton's anger. "Under the stairs," he prompted. "Did you ever see what was down there?"

"N-no, why—? What has that got to do with anything?" Michael turned to Violet, expression softening.

She was pale, tears glistening in her eyes, staring unseeingly at the floor. Her hands shook as she fiddled with her hair, her breaths tiny hiccups. She wouldn't look at any of them. "Vi?" Ashton leant towards her, fingers brushing on her knee. She jolted, startling away from him.

"I mean you no upset, Violet," Michael promised. "Yachtman used that basement to study mutant genetics," he told Ashton. "He invented weapons and forms of incarceration, all designed to face us. We... we've lost friends to that basement. You almost lost your sister to it too." Michael's brow furrowed, eyes dark with grief. Finn was silent, oddly still and solemn. "He needed to test those weapons. And who better to test them on than the mutant

64

trapped under his roof?"

Ashton's temper flared once more.

"Then why—?"

"We sabotaged his work. Deleted files, messed with his inventions. Stole a lot of his data too. We've got some pretty good hackers here." Michael shifted, gesturing to Ashton to hold off on yelling for another minute. "We cannot move directly against him. He is one of the most powerful people in the country. What we *can* do, without losing anyone else, is break down his work from the inside. We've got spies – human spies – in the AMCD. We had spies, mutant and human, hosting parties and blatantly inviting him, just so someone else could get into that basement."

Michael tucked his pen behind his ear. "We knew of Violet when she first showed her powers. That football went in Brenda's garden, she saw the whole thing. We elected to keep an eye on things at first. I mean, a mutant born to a human family. How? Why? Was it something Yachtman did? We needed more answers first." He shared a look with Finn before continuing. "You lived on that street because we wanted you to. The whole thing was a trap for Yachtman; *I* sold him that house. He has been looking for this place since I was a kid. Could you imagine his face when he realises what we did? We've been right under his nose this whole time and he was none the wiser."

"How were you going to trap him?"

"He's killing us. Actively trying to hunt us to extinction. We will do whatever we can, but like I said, we must safeguard our people. We can only do so much. We wanted him somewhere we could keep an eye on him, and it was working. Until Violet was born." Finn sat up, stretching.

"Here's the deal," Finn said, spreading his hands, "if we

barged in and took Violet as soon as we found out about her—Yachtman would twig we were spying on him, and he'd stop at nothing to find us. Everything we had worked for would be gone. Then… then you all got older and if we took her then, he'd suspect one of you. Well, *you* specifically." He nodded at Ashton. "And we knew she wouldn't leave without you. Our safest bet was for you to get the both of you out of there. Then he can't pin it on us and kill us and you could be free to do whatever you thought right."

"We knew you were out. Brenda told us." Michael picked up the story. "Paul and Kurtis were one of the teams we had looking for you. We would offer help, in any form, and see what your decision would be thereafter." He looked at Violet again. "Do you need a minute?"

"He's horrible," she sniffled.

"He is," Michael agreed. "But he can't get you or your brother here. He'll never find this place."

"How can you be sure?" Ashton pressed.

"See, Mike's clever," Finn smirked. "The only way Yachtman can find out is if Michael himself tells him. Everyone else can try, but they'll never be able to send him in the right direction. They'll forget where we are or he'll take a wrong turn or, in some cases, he'll stand right outside and see *nothing*."

"Nothing?"

"*Nothing*."

"Do, uh, do people often tell him where you are?"

"No, but…" Michael sighed. "The information can come out under torture."

"Oh." Ashton bit his lip. "I'm… sorry."

No one said anything for a moment. Finn and Michael seemed to be having a silent discussion. Ashton turned to his sister. Her hair was beginning to frizz from where she was braiding it.

He leant over, waving to catch her attention. "Are you all right?" he asked softly.

She dropped her hands, the plait unravelling slowly of its own accord. "Do you want to take a break?" he asked.

She met his gaze. Something in her eyes, eyes so much like his, squished something in his chest. He wanted to ask— what had happened in that basement?

"—can get Stephen to bugger up the boiler." Finn was saying, his and Michael's heads bowed towards each other, talking in murmurs. "Then put him on hold to get it 'fixed'." The air quotes came with a sly grin. Michael rolled his eyes.

"I meant in terms of these two."

"You never specified."

"I thought it was obvious."

"You thought wrong."

"Clearly," Michael sighed. Finn dug his elbow into Michael's ribs, jostling him. "Violet. Do you need anything?"

"Drink. Please," she requested in a small voice. Finn snapped his fingers and a glass appeared on the floor beside her feet alongside a ceramic pitcher of iced water. She reached for it instantly.

"How does that work?" Ashton puzzled, snapping his fingers too. Violet began taking small sips of water.

"A magician never reveals their secrets." Finn replied haughtily. It was Michael's turn to elbow him.

"We can discuss abilities later. Today's talk was to bring you two up to speed and discuss your next move. You are more than welcome to stay here if you wish. We can work to understand each other, answer any questions you may have and teach Violet to control her powers. If you want to leave, we will send you off with whatever resources you need and can recommend several safe locations for you." The siblings exchanged looks. "A decision doesn't need to be made now. You can stay as long as you like."

"What is this place?" Violet asked.

"We call it the Haven. Finn calls it the Hovel—"

"I'm charming like that."

"—most of us just call it home."

"Ugh, you old sop."

"I've been 'big boss', as Finn calls it, for about eight years now. Before me, it was my uncle, may he rest in peace."

"See, I told you. Nepotism."

"Shush, you menace."

"Rude."

"We're not the only place like this in the world, but we are the biggest. Mutants are welcome here and they are safe here. They find homes, jobs, friends and family. We teach them how to control their powers, teach them to look after themselves, to be safe." Ashton looked around the room again. The sheer number of pens alone would have easily cost him his yearly wages.

Michael smiled at him, giving the impression he could see right into Ashton's mind. "I did mention I sell homes to rich people, didn't I?"

"That's the best bit," Finn grinned. "Mike's a clever clogs money bags, but rather than being a *complete* snob, he helps us ratty lot."

"Don't let Kathy hear you say that," Michael warned good-naturedly. "She won't much appreciate being called 'ratty'."

"How many people are there? Living here?" Ashton clarified, albeit unnecessarily.

68

"Mm." Michael grimaced. "There are about... four thousand of us? Give or take." He raised an eyebrow at Finn, who shrugged. "We have room for about ten thousand, *but*," he huffed, "we never get there."

Ashton almost asked why, but the look the pair were giving them was more than enough.

Finn gave a tight smile.

"Well, you're all boring me now." He saluted. "Ta-ra." He vanished, the beanbags shifting at the sudden disappearance of his weight.

"Yes, I think that is enough for today. Not because you're boring me," Michael promised, holding his hands up placatingly. "Bit of information overload, isn't it?"

The siblings nodded.

Michael added, "Take the rest of the day. You're more than welcome to drop by tomorrow morning, should you have any questions. I believe Kathy set a room up for you on Floor Five. Ask for Garry with two Rs."

Michael saw them out. He shook Violet's hand first, smiling again. "It's nice to finally meet you. My door is always open. Figuratively. Must keep the heat in."

Then to Ashton, shaking his hand too. The tingle was not as sudden this time, but it was there, wriggling uncertainly somewhere in his forearm. "If there's any trouble, get me or Finn on the comms. I hope there isn't trouble, but you are the only human who's ever been allowed in and you're Yachtman's son, no less."

"I didn't ask to be," Ashton grumbled.

"And on that," Michael let go, the tingle vanished, "I feel your pain. Now, do excuse me. Chapter thirty-seven has been calling me."

Chapter Seven

They got back to Floor Five with relative ease, although someone on Floor Six tried to give them a handful of frogspawn to deliver to Finn. Ashton politely grossed out, grabbing Violet's hand and hurrying down the stairs.

"He had that in his *pocket*!" he whispered, grimacing. Violet nodded in agreement, equally disgusted. "Um, excuse me." Ashton waved to someone wandering past. "Oh, I know you."

"Yep." Kurtis grinned. "How's it going, mate? Aww, look at you!" Kurtis beamed, squishing Violet's face in his hands. "You look much better! You feeling OK?"

"Man had frogspawn." she managed, tapping his hand to free her face.

"Oh, that's Ryan. He always has frogspawn." Kurtis snorted. "How'd it go with Michael?"

"Mm." Ashton made a face. "We have to look for—"

"Garry with two Rs? Mate, we're gonna be neighbours!" He messed Violet's hair, laughing. "Garry's this way, come on."

Garry with two Rs was easily the tallest, most muscular man Ashton had ever seen outside of anime. He towered over everyone, seven and a half feet tall easily and proportionately wide with muscles Ashton didn't even know existed. His jaw was undoubtedly a brick, his tan skin was criss-crossed with scars on every bit of exposed skin. Bald, eyebrows dropped in a seemingly permanent glower, storm-grey eyes surveying the hall for any minute discrepancy.

"No running!" he boomed. A trio of teenagers slowed to a meek walk, even their conversation slowing to whispers.

"Hey, G!" Kurtis waved, arm extended overhead to catch the giant's attention. "Got some newbies for you."

"Michael send 'em?"

"Yep." Kurtis turned to wave Ashton and Violet forward. The siblings were too stunned to move, gawping up at this gargantuan man. "This is Ashton and Violet. Give them a minute."

Garry didn't wait, stomping forward until he was less than a foot from them both. He stared down his nose at them, a scowl on his lips. Ashton dared not move. Garry's gaze was as heavy as the man himself.

"You Yachtman's boy?"

"Y-yes, sir."

"Mmph," Garry grunted, "heard you got him good."

"Wow." Kurtis marvelled at Ashton. "You made *Garry* laugh. *Wow*."

Ashton blinked. Violet's expression mirrored his own confusion, but he didn't get a chance to say anything. Garry clapped him on the shoulder, almost putting him through the wall.

Ashton's back slid down the surface until he was sitting on the floor, winded and a bit bruised.

"Oops." Garry scruffed Ashton, hauling him up and setting him back down beside Violet. "You humans are too light."

"I've heard," Ashton wheezed. Violet gripped his arm, studying his face. "I'm OK." He offered a smile, tucking her hair behind her ear.

"This way." Garry jerked his head. "I'll try not to acquaint you with the masonry again."

"I'll appreciate it." Ashton nodded, rubbing his ribs. Garry grunted again. Kurtis spluttered protest.

"*Twice!*" he squealed. "Made him laugh *twice!* Ooooh," he narrowed his eyes at Ashton, "that's witchcraft."

"Um… I hate to point out the logic there, but…" he winced, splaying his hand to indicate Kurtis, Garry, the mutants around him.

"Still witchcraft."

Their room was number five hundred and sixteen, with a green door. Violet brightened at the colour. Garry gave her the key, a bright silver thing he made her promise to look after. She nodded seriously, sliding the key into the lock.

Kurtis was still with them, wedging himself shoulder-to-shoulder with Ashton to see their room too.

He pouted up at Garry. "How come their room's nicer than mine?"

"There's two of 'em, so they get more space. And you're a slob."

"Am not."

"Tell that to the socks that can walk themselves to the laundry room."

"Don't know what you're talking about," Kurtis mumbled. He turned to the newcomers, finally noticing the pair had moved into the room.

It was easily twice as big as Ashton's room back home. A large window took up most of the wall opposite the door, framed by emerald-green blackout curtains. On either side, two single beds neatly made up with plain, white bedding. The carpet was a soft grey. There was a large wardrobe to the left of the door, a chest of drawers on the other side with a mirror above it. On the right-hand wall, a desk with only a pen pot and a thick notepad. On the left wall, a broad bookcase filled to bursting with a range of novels. Two squishy green beanbags were stationed on either side of it.

"Wow," Ashton said. There was a faint smell of something oceanic in here. He spotted a reed diffuser on the windowsill.

"Yeah, we're pretty comfy here," Kurtis smiled, "what do you think, kiddo?"

He grinned at Violet. She blinked at him, fingers curled around the key. Her gaze slid to her brother, confusion knitting her brow. Ashton crouched, resting a hand on her shoulder.

"Which bed do you want? Left or right?"

"I don't—" she mumbled. A nervous glance at Garry, re-evaluating his ginormous stature, ducking her head. Ashton started to speak, stopping when she began pulling on her hair, twisting it between her fingers.

"It's not going to be like before," he said gently. He curled his fingers lightly around the hand that held the key. "This is your room, OK? We could... we could find you some nice bedding if that's all right with Garry?"

He half-turned to squint up at the giant—his face was *somewhere* up there.

"You can have whatever bedding you want. Just don't set it on fire."

"Fire?" Violet echoed.

"Hot stuff. Glows. Gives me a ton of paperwork. I hate *paperwork*." He snarled the word, like there couldn't possibly be anything worse.

"He sets it on fire," Kurtis supplied.

Garry cut him a look. Kurtis laughed nervously. "Yay on your new room, OK, byyyyeeeee!"

He vanished out the door so quickly, no one was sure if he had ported or sprinted.

"Idiot," Garry sighed. "Anyway, I'll let you two get settled. The rules," he flung his hand out to indicate a laminated poster on the back of the door, "are simple. Kurtis can show you the communal areas later. See this?"

He pointed to a metal box beside the door. It had one blue button beneath a round speaker. "This is the comms system. Like a walkie-talkie without the walkie. Every room and hallway has one and yes, that does mean everyone can hear you. Mostly used to find people, pass on messages, start drama, the works. OK? OK." He nodded to them both in turn, closing the door behind him.

"So, Vi," Ashton smiled, "left or right?"

***

It made no sense. David realised that over dinner, but now he dwelled on it. Sat alone in the basement, the only light from the computer screen in front of him. He leant back in his chair, hands folded on his stomach. He swayed in the chair, turning a fraction to the left, then mirroring the move to the right.

It made no sense at all.

The beast was as good as dead. His son only marginally better off. A cheap shot had allowed them to escape. Anger burned around his ribcage. *A cheap shot.*

He had teams looking for them. Highly trained soldiers of the AMCD, trained under the protocols he himself wrote. They had hunted down more mutants than they could want. Why could they not find one lousy human?

He hadn't told them about the mutant masquerading as his own flesh and blood. God above, no. He would lose everything. He gave them a story, one of Ashton's weak will and weaker stomach pushing him out the door and away from his future as David's successor.

It made no sense.

His son had taken *nothing*. No money, no clothes but the ones on his back, no food, no *shoes* so hastily did he leave. What was his plan? Succumb to a life on the streets? There was no family in the area. No hospital or veterinary surgery he could beg for help—David's men were ready, waiting.

It had been over twenty-four hours now. Ashton should have been found. The freak was undoubtedly dead.

David smiled to himself, feeling the echo of the hammer shattering bone wriggling through his hand.

He had done less to mutants thrice its size and power, had seen better, more final results. Of course, it was dead. Inexplicably born as the abomination it was, a tarnish, a blight on his career, his very existence, but so unbearably disappointing.

A natural-born mutant? To human parents? Unheard of. A miracle. A curse.

But it was weak. His gaze passed along the top of the monitor. The array of screens sparked, webbed with smashes and cracks. His hammer remained in one of them. A shard of glass had cut the side of his hand. He did not feel it, watching the blood drip with detached fascination. He looked past the monitors to the stairs. To the brick at the base of the stairs' construction. A laugh coiled in his throat, a *humph* of bemusement.

It was dead. But he could still use it.

***

Ashton was still awake come midnight. He sat up in his new bed, the room dimly lit by the moon. It was warm. It was comfortable. He felt like Goldilocks, in the bed that was just right. And yet... sleep refused to visit him.

Not that he wasn't tired. His eyes prickled with exhaustion; someone had replaced his brain with jelly. He couldn't decide if his bones were still in place either, his body ignored every command his jelly brain sluggishly tried to give out.

He could see Violet, just about. Her outline, more to the point, tucked under the bedding. It had taken over an hour to get her to accept the bed was hers. Another half an hour of Kurtis reiterating that Yachtman could not find them here. Then ten minutes of tucking her in repeatedly.

"Just lie down," Ashton had said, pushing lightly on her shoulder.

"But—"

"You need sleep. Lie down."

She kicked the duvet away, swinging her feet out. Ashton caught her around the middle for the umpteenth time, hauling her back onto the bed and throwing the quilt over her again. "Vi—Vi—*Violet*!"

She froze, her eyes fixing on something past his ear.

Ashton sighed. "Just making sure you're listening. Lie down."

"But—it's..." Her eyes flitted over the crumpled bedding, rubbing her thumb across her finger. "It's not right."

76

"You're right." Ashton nodded. "It's *not* right that you're nine and only just getting a proper bed. Now, will you *please* lie down? You can have cake for breakfast if you *just* lie down."

"What kind of cake?"

"Biggest, chocolatiest piece I can find," he promised, nodding earnestly. "But only if you go to sleep. Right now."

That had worked, the promise of cake. Ashton hoped he could actually find said promised cake come the morning, but that, he decided, was a future-Ashton problem.

Present-Ashton was dealing with something else.

He was pondering whether or not Violet had actually had cake before when he noticed that, after *finally* lying down and going to sleep, she was not sleeping very well. It began as shifting, rolling onto her side and then the other. Then she started mumbling, too quiet and fragmented for him to make out.

She rolled onto her back, shaking her head, squashing the pillow over her ears. Ashton threw his quilt off, sliding from his bed to crouch beside hers.

"Vi." He squeezed her arm, shaking her lightly. "Vi, wake up."

She whimpered, turning her face away. He pulled on the pillow, gently prying her fingers from it. He called for her again, wriggling the pillow away from her right ear. He brushed her hair back from her forehead, giving her another shake.

Her breathing hitched. Tears fell, falling back into her hair, and she began to cry. Ashton gave up on the shaking, rising and taking hold of her shoulders, making her sit up. The movement disturbed her. She awoke with a start, catching a yelp in her hand. Upon seeing him, she welled up and slumped, sobbing, into his shoulder. "I've got you," he murmured, her fingers curling into the back of his T-shirt. "I've got you."

She was shivering. Ashton reached around her to wrap her up in the duvet, kissing the top of her head. "You want to talk about it?"

He felt her shake her head, still trembling. She sniffed, wiping her eyes on the bedding. He adjusted the duvet, hugging her to him with a squeeze, rubbing circles onto her back.

It was a few minutes before she could get words out, her voice shaking almost as much as she was.

"Y-you're gr-grey."

"Um, excuse you. I'm hoping not to go grey for another fifty years, at least."

A hiccup shook her shoulders, she turned her face up, frowning at him. He smiled apologetically, touching her cheek, wiping a stray tear away with his thumb. "What does grey mean then?"

"Mm. Sad?" she grimaced, looking down again and squashing her cheek on his chest. "Not sad-sad, but…" She fumbled for an explanation, eventually hunching her shoulders.

"I'm worried," he admitted. "Could that be it?"

Her head wobbled indecisively; he saw her hand come up to play with a lock of hair.

"I'm sorry," she mumbled.

"You've got nothing to apologise for."

"I make you worry."

"I'm your big brother. Course I'm going to worry."

"Sorry."

"Stop apologising."

"Sorry."

"Oh my God."

"Sorry."

"I will smother you," he warned, clamping a hand over her mouth when he saw yet another 'sorry' coming up. "Stop it. You only say sorry when you've actually got something to say sorry for. OK?"

She nodded. "If I let go," Ash warned playfully, "and you say sorry again, I'll eat your cake for the rest of our lives. Every slice you get, it will be *mine*. Yes?" She nodded again. He let go, watching her carefully. He could see the apology building, saw her eyes shift, saw her bite the inside of her cheek. He raised an eyebrow at her, and she bowed her head onto his shoulder. "Yeah," he said, patting her head, "I love you too."

Chapter Eight

Kurtis and Paul knocked on the door about eight the following morning. Ashton and Violet were awake, had been since six. They had eventually drifted back to sleep, squashed in her bed. Now, he was reading to her, bringing her up to speed on all the books she had missed back home.

"*Harry Potter* is a classic," he told her, slipping from the bed to answer the door.

"The author…" Kurtis grimaced upon the door opening, "not so much."

Violet frowned, bewildered. Kurtis flapped a hand. "I'll explain later," he said. "I like berating people on a full stomach, so come on! Chop-chop!"

"You don't stand between Kurtis and his bacon." Paul smiled.

"No, you most certainly do not." Kurtis grinned.

The duo led the siblings to the ground floor, chatting away, introducing them to mutants, pointing out things to them, piling Violet with a list of books and films they thought was a travesty she hadn't read or seen yet.

"*Star Wars,*" Paul said. Kurtis glared at him.

"*Star Trek!*"

"*Star Wars!*"

"*Trek!*"

"*Wars!*"

"*Shrek!*" Finn appeared from nowhere, shoving the

squabbling pair apart. He put his hands on his hips, looking down at Violet. "You *have* to watch *Shrek*, or we just won't be friends any more. Here, have a lolly." He smiled, pressing three green ones into her hand. "Breakfast first though," he hastily pressed on, "breakfast is the most important meal of the day."

"You always have sweets for breakfast." Kurtis puzzled. Paul nudged him and pointed. Ashton looked over his shoulder, seeing Kathy fifteen feet away and glaring daggers at her colleague.

"No, no!" Finn laughed nervously, picking Violet up and hurrying into the cafeteria. "I always have a full, varied meal for breakfast. With, uh, with some fruit and some milk. There you go."

He set Violet down, putting his hands on his knees to lean down and be eye level with her. "You will have your five a day, young lady, or Kathy will kill me. Clear?"

She nodded, sending a befuddled look past him to Ashton. Finn smiled. "Good girl. Have a lolly."

"FINNIGAN!"

"I'm not here!" Finn vanished, reappearing further away, safely hidden behind Garry with two Rs, who subsequently put him in a headlock.

The cafeteria was by far the biggest room they had seen yet. Michael had said ten thousand could be at home here. They saw that now, approximately four thousand people in a space built for more than twice that much. By no means, though, did the room seem empty. It was bright and cheerful and rang with laughter and bickering and the chink of cutlery. Hundreds and hundreds of tables with hundreds and hundreds more chairs, set out without any order, pulled together in places; pushed to the walls in others and some were abandoned in the middle of nowhere. None of the furniture matched. No one really seemed to care. The walls were a pastel-mint, almost cream under the lights. The floor was well-worn wood, but still solid. Along the back wall, spanning the width of the cafeteria, was a buffet. Scents of toast and bacon and sausages made Ashton's stomach grumble.

A hand on his arm, Violet looking up at him, clutching her four lollipops. Kurtis threw an arm around Ashton's shoulders, grinning.

"Where'd you want to sit, neighbour?"

They picked a table nearer to the wall, as close to the buffet as they could get. Violet sat on the outside of the table, taking care to line her sweets up in perfect parallel lines. Ashton sat beside her, Paul and Kurtis dragging chairs in to sit opposite them.

"What do you want to eat, Vi?"

"Me?"

"You're the only Vi I know," Ashton confirmed. "Want to go have a look?"

"We'll hold the table." Paul grinned, indicating Kurtis with a nod. Ashton held his hand out. Violet glanced sidelong at her lollies once more, then took her brother's hand.

They found pancakes, available with more toppings than Ashton had ever seen—cream, sugar, chocolate and syrup to jelly beans, custard creams and strawberry yoghurt. Pancakes, he argued, may not have been chocolate cake, but they still had cake in the name. Violet wrinkled her nose at him, surveying the weirder topping choices.

"We are an odd bunch."

Ashton turned at the voice.

Michael smiled at him, loading his plate up with pancakes. "Morning. Morning, Violet. Sleep well?"

"We're reading *Harry Potter*," Violet supplied, flicking her hands.

Michael's smile brightened.

"You have a favourite character yet?" he asked, burying his breakfast in whipped cream and syrup.

"Cat lady." Violet nodded, frowning as the name slipped her mind.

"McGonagall," Ashton said helpfully.

"You have good taste." Michael nodded, upturning the jelly bean jar over his plate.

"Can't say the same about you." Ashton nodded, staring at the monstrosity meal. Michael shrugged a shoulder, still smiling. Ash shook his head and turned to his sister. "What are you having, Vi?"

She pointed at Michael's plate in question. Ashton moved her hand to point at a nearby fruit bowl. She tried pointing with her other hand, but he caught that too. Michael laughed, setting the jar down.

"Listen to your brother, miss. Breakfast like this, you'll have no teeth by the time you're ten."

Someone cleared their throat. Michael winced, turning and hunching his shoulders innocently. "Morning, Kathy. I was just—"

"Overdosing on sugar?" She arched an eyebrow, arms folded, leaning on her hip. Michael grimaced. "Honestly, you and Finn are *terrible*. It's a miracle your arteries aren't clogged up with gelatine." She snapped her fingers. The fruit bowl zipped towards them, losing a few grapes. She tipped her chin up at Michael. He sighed, defeated, and took a banana.

Kathy sent him away, glowering at his jelly-bean breakfast. Michael sat on the other side of Garry, who had apparently killed Finn as he was nowhere in sight.

The medic whipped back round. "And you," she wagged a finger at Violet, "you *will* have a proper breakfast. Sweets are for treats."

The medic stayed with them for another ten minutes, checking what they picked up, their fruit intake, making sure they had milk and examining their portion sizes.

Ashton ended up with a full English breakfast and an orange. Violet had pancakes with chocolate spread and banana pieces and a big glass of milk that Kathy carried back to the table for her.

She saw the lollies immediately, sighing. "You can have *one* today," she stressed, tapping the sweet on Violet's nose. "And if Finn tries to give you more, tell him to put a quid in the Sugar Jar, OK?"

"OK."

"Good girl. Eat your breakfast."

Paul and Kurtis ventured off for their food once the siblings were seated. Kurtis' plate was ninety-eight percent bacon and bacon sandwiches. Paul had beans on toast with grated cheese on top.

"Bea made the pancakes today," Paul informed them. "Their pancakes are the *best*."

He eyed Violet's plate almost enviously. She looked up from cutting into the stack, staring at him. "I won't steal them," he hurriedly assured, holding his hands up. Beside him, Kurtis chuckled.

Ashton kept an eye on Violet while they ate. He could not remember the last time she had had a proper meal. The thought

84

drew his attention to her wrists—had they always been so thin?

She was quiet, but rather enjoying her food. She had chocolate on her cheek. She reached for her drink, holding the glass carefully in both hands, eyes travelling around the room as she drank. Ashton dipped toast into his fried egg, shaking his head when Paul swiped some of Kurtis' bacon. Kurtis froze, only his eyes moving to fume at his friend sidelong. Paul looked everywhere but the seat next to him.

Violet made a funny little squeaking noise. Her glass slipped from her fingers, shattering on the floor. The colour drained from her face, suddenly stiff.

A cheer went up around them, as one often does at a breakage in a setting like this. She flinched, turning to Ashton with tears in her eyes.

"Hey," Kurtis leant forward, "no use crying over spilt milk." He grinned.

Ashton threw a forkful of baked beans at him, the mess splattering over his nose and cheek. "Mmph. Rude."

"We'll clean it up, Vi," Ashton comforted, gently easing her hand away from pulling on her hair, "no problem."

He made to stand, but Paul waved him down.

"No need," he said, motioning again for Ashton to sit. With a wave of his hand, the broken glass vanished, taking the puddle of milk with it. Kurtis snapped his fingers and a fresh one appeared in front of Violet. She stared at it, sniffing, trembling. "Honestly, if we had a penny for everything that got broken in this place, we could... uh what takes a lot of money?"

"Billionaires," Kurtis grunted, cleaning his face on a napkin. Paul snorted in bemusement.

"You get the idea," he said.

"Everyone OK?"

Michael was there, Finn at his shoulder. The question went to all at the table, but he was looking at Violet. Seeing her shake, his expression softened and he leant down. "Are you hurt?"

She shook her head, hastily wiping at her eyes. Michael smiled kindly. "Good," he said, "glasses and milk are easily replaced. You," he poked her in the arm, "are not. It was an accident, no one was hurt, and it's all cleaned up now. Yes?"

She hiccupped, nodding. Finn squished his way in, flicking his hand and providing her a box of tissues.

"I'm sorry."

"You have nothing to apologise for."

"See, Vi?" Ashton nudged her. "Told you."

She gave a weak smile, squashing the tissue to her nose. "Thank you." he said, looking to the four mutants. "Thank you."

"We're here for each other." Michael squeezed Violet's shoulder, but also partially used her as leverage to stand. "Why don't you and your brother pop by my office when you're done here?"

"Can I come?" Finn interrupted. Michael opened his mouth to respond but pointed at something past Finn. Six tables away, Kathy and Jeevan were glaring at their colleague. Finn grumbled. "Bloody stocktake. I *hate* stocktake. Kurtis will do it for me, won't you, Kurt—? You've got sauce on your nose."

"No, I don't."

"Right there. You grub."

"Ashton threw beans at me!"

"You deserved it."

86

"Did he say, 'no use crying over spilt milk'?"

"*Yes.*"

"That will never be funny, Kurtis. And you've *still* got sauce on your nose!" Kurtis threw down his napkin.

"Maybe I'll start a trend then!"

"I seriously doubt that."

***

They sat by the fire this time. The flames were a metallic-turquoise today. Violet was watching them dance, gaze distant. Ashton sat in the armchair to her right, Michael to her left. He had made tea for himself and Ashton, now sipping his. He stretched his legs out, pushing his heels on the rug.

"I love this chair," he said. "Get some of my best thinking done here."

Ashton nodded politely, turning his cup in his hands. Michael turned to him. "How are you finding things so far?"

"Someone got glued to a chair," Ashton replied nonchalantly. Michael gave a snort of laughter, a wicked smile hurriedly quashed.

"Mm, yes. I heard. Poor Sara."

"And some weirdo had jelly bean pancakes for breakfast."

"Don't bash it 'til you try it." Michael stuck his tongue out. Ashton looked down at his tea, tapping his fingers on his mug. "And what about you, Violet?" Michael asked. "Besides reading?"

She didn't respond, still engrossed in the fire. It burned tall and bright, exuding a steady, comfortable heat.

Michael leant forward a fraction. "Violet?"

She gave a little start, head whipping round.

Michael smiled at her, that kindly smile he could summon like a breath. "You OK?" A funny motion between a nod and a shake, his smile picked up understanding. "I've spilt enough milk to stock an ASDA, you will never be worse than me. And you have full permission to ignore Kurtis if you want to."

The corners of her mouth tipped up for a split second. Michael sat back, took another sip of tea. "What did you see?"

The question hung in the air for a moment, wafting on the warmth. The fire snapped; the turquoise chased away by a mauve. Michael's gaze lingered on the colour change for a moment, then slid to Violet. She was running the ends of her hair between her thumb and finger.

Ashton bit his lip, trying to keep his tea steady. There was a look in Michael's eye, something simultaneously inquisitive and knowledgeable as he tipped his head, holding his mug in steepled fingers.

Unexpectedly, Michael stayed quiet, shifting in his chair and focusing on the flames. Violet looked at her brother, shoulders hunching.

"What do you mean?" Ashton asked. Michael got through half his tea before offering up answers.

"Abilities stretch across a vast expanse of creation. All mutants have inborn abilities—heightened senses, increased strength, blah blah blah. Then there's secondary abilities." He drained the last of his tea, set the cup on the floor by his feet. "For example, Finn has incredible healing abilities, probably some of the most advanced in recorded history. If he could only get a bedside manner to match, he could be the greatest doctor on the planet." He snapped his fingers, holding his hand up as if expecting a high five.

Ashton was ready to oblige out of social conduct when a book flew over his head, its spine lining up with Michael's outstretched palm. Violet stared at it, awed. "Yep," he smiled, "summoning objects is something you can learn."

"Like milk."

"Yes, eventually. Summoning seen and unseen objects are widely different, but we'll go over that later." He set the book down in his lap, opening to the contents page. The book had worn, yellowed pages, the hardback cover was once black but now faded and well-read. There was no title. The text was handwritten. "You saw something at breakfast, didn't you? You were startled and dropped the glass. What did you see?" He raised his head, awaiting her reply, keeping his eyes trained on the pages as he flicked through. Violet considered the fire, inhaling slowly. Ashton set his tea down unfinished, resting his elbow on his knee.

"Vi?" He touched her arm. She flexed her fingers, looking around as though the information she needed would be somewhere around the fireplace.

"There's no rush," Michael said calmly, stopping about halfway through the book and running his finger down the page. "I have a pretty good idea anyway, but it's for you to tell me."

"Idea?" Ashton echoed.

"A thought that can be helpful."

"I *know*—you do that on purpose."

"Ah, it's second nature. I grew up with Finn." He shrugged a shoulder.

"I was hoping you'd *elaborate* on this 'pretty good idea' of yours," Ashton grumbled. Michael sent him a sideways smirk, but it was clear he would not progress the conversation until Violet did.

The only sound in the office for a solid, few minutes was the snaps and crackles of the fire. It was still purple, although not as deeply so, flickering with its previous colour. Michael was still reading, turning the pages back and forth, lips moving in soundless thought.

Violet sniffed, letting go of her hair to tuck her hands between her knees.

"Colours. I see colours." A beat and then her cheeks flushed crimson. "I-I mean, I... I see... there's like..." She waved her hand in front of her. The fire flashed, shrunk for a moment, and then jumped back up, now a deep red. Violet sat back in her chair, slumping.

"Do you mean you see colours that other people don't?" Michael suggested. She hummed uncertainly. Ashton caught her eye, saw her give a small nod.

"She can tell how I'm feeling," he said carefully, keeping an eye on her, gauging her reactions. "Blue is sad. We think grey is worried."

"Do you see the colours around people or over people?"

"Um... around?"

"Do you see colours in relation to senses?"

"N-no, but... er..." Her brow creased, hands curling into the hem of her shirt. "Loud hurts."

"Does loud have a colour?"

"Hot."

"Do I have a colour?" Michael cocked his head again. At some point, he had summoned a pen and a notepad, scribbling away. Violet watched the pen move in his left hand, eyes travelling up his arm, to his head, and then studying the air around him.

"Yellow."

"Any particular yellow?"

"Uh..." She squinted, picking at her lip. "Like... ooh, trumpet flowers." Michael's pen froze and he laughed.

"*What* flowers?" He asked, amusement twinkling in his rich-brown, amber-speckled eyes.

"*Daffodils*," Ashton translated, realising he had blurted the word. "Uh, daffodils," he repeated in a more controlled tone, looking away as Michael smiled again.

"I like daffodils," he said.

Violet nodded, going cross-eyed to make a tiny plait before her face. Michael twisted his pen between his fingers. "Is yellow good?"

"Yes."

"Is it happy?"

"No." She shook her head.

"What is it? Do you know?"

"Mm." She dropped her hair, rubbing her ears. "It's, um… it's like…" She fumbled for a moment, humming. "Curious." She eventually decided. "But in… in a nice way."

"What's curious in a bad way?"

"Brown. Brownish-yellow." Michael wrote a little more, then stopped, pen poised over the paper. Violet was curling her hair around her forefinger, staring at the fire once again, expression moulding into something unreadable. She tucked her hands under her legs.

"What's wrong?" Ashton worried, reaching out to tuck her hair behind her ear. He saw her eyes shimmer with firelight. He knew. She didn't need to say it, he just knew. "That's the colour he had. Wasn't it?"

She nodded. Michael waved his hand, a tissue box plopping into her lap. She took one on reflex, but rather than wipe her eyes, she began folding it at random intervals. She sniffed, blinked. The tissue trembled in her fingers.

"OK to carry on?" Michael pressed gently, doodling something on his paper. Violet started folding a second tissue, the first fluttering to the floor. He waited for her to nod. "How many colours have you seen?"

"Lots."

"Do you know what they all mean?"

"Sort of."

"Go on." He urged, pen at the ready.

Violet pressed her fingertips together, watching them tent.

"Blue is sad," she mumbled. "Yellow is curious. Grey is worried."

"What's red, do you know that one?"

"Embarrassed."

"Green?"

"Scared."

"White?"

"Lying."

"Black?"

"Secret."

"Mm… What's brown on its own?"

Violet frowned, plucking another tissue.

"Mean."

"Do different shades mean anything? Say, is a darker green more scared than a lighter green?" Violet bobbed her head, neither a yes nor a no. Michael wrote something else. "You said you saw brownish-yellow. Have you seen any other combinations?"

"Grey and blue."

"Who?"

"Ash." Violet turned to her brother with an almost guilty look.

"Is he still blue and grey?"

"Ish."

"Ish?" Ashton stayed stock still while she inspected him.

He glanced surreptitiously at his hand, but, of course, he saw no colours beyond the ordinary.

"He's gone a bit pink. Tiny bit." She circled a finger at him, squinting. "Tiny, tiny bit."

"What's pink?"

"Don't know. It's new."

"Is it good?" Ashton tried to keep his tone level, but he wasn't sure how he felt about having a 'new' colour. He remained motionless under her gaze. She picked at her shirt, humming in thought as she studied his face.

"Think so." She nodded, Michael mimicking the motion, still writing away. He crossed something out, pen scratching, and then continued, jotting down more than she had said.

Ashton waited until he stopped.

"Is this part of your 'pretty good idea'?"

"Mm-hm." Michael confirmed, tapping the pen on his chin.

The book had been on his lap, under his writing. He swapped the two, returning to his page quickly, having dog-eared it. It took him almost a minute to realise the siblings were staring at him expectantly. "Mm? Oh. Right. Um..." He tapped the pen on his chin. "Have you always seen the colours, Violet?" She nodded. "On everyone?" Another nod, he wrote something else. "One more—what did you see at breakfast?"

She tensed, knee jiggling. She laced her fingers and looked down, hair framing her face. Michael tucked his pen behind his ear, sliding his notes into the book. "I need to find some stuff," he said. "Check some things over. I'll try to catch up with you at dinner. Is that OK?"

Chapter Nine

They couldn't exactly say no, so they found themselves rambling around the place. They got a bit lost somewhere on Floor Two and ended up traipsing down a hundred and thirty-six stairs – they counted – and found themselves outside in a field of a garden. Trees of all shapes and sizes with names neither of them really knew framed the expanse of frosted green grass and shrubberies. Flowerbeds were a little sparse, there was a rather large pond rippling under a willow tree; a seating area beside it stashed under a wooden shelter with another pink fire dancing in a metal brazier in the middle. People were sitting there, laughing and joking. One of them was juggling with the fire, flashes of pink, blazing orbs wildly ricocheting from hand to hand.

There were paths ground into the dirt, worn down by walking, quite suited to the surroundings. Children were playing, screaming and roaring and shrieking with delight. One of them shrank into a mouse, tumbled into a forward roll and came back up as herself. Her friends carried on running and she bounded after them without a second thought.

Ashton raised an eyebrow at Violet.

"Can you do that?"

She just stared back at him, unimpressed. Ashton laughed, messing her hair. "Ooh, we probably should find you a hairbrush. Tie this wig up." He looked back the way they had come; grey stone steps up to the large, wooden door. It had symbols painted onto it, ones that glowed in various shades of orange. "Let's go back in. Bit taters out here."

She nodded in agreement, tucking her tangled hair behind her ears. She took Ashton's hand and followed quietly.

They attempted to retrace their steps, finding the killer staircase. A single look and they decided against climbing that monstrosity. They carried on instead.

Floor Two, it seemed, held those with elemental-based powers. A man walked past them, gills on his neck, head and shoulders encased in an undulating sphere of water. He had webbed hands too, revealing this when he waved and smiled at them.

Someone was entertaining a gaggle of toddlers with burst of flames that took on animalistic shapes. There was a game of rock-paper-scissors underway, a real rock bursting from the wall when they lost. They chased their friend down the hallway, yelling in Italian.

A hand caught Ashton by the arm, making him nearly jump out of his skin. He whirled around, fist clenched in panic, pushing Violet behind him.

"Whoa!" Sara laughed, hands up in surrender, "easy now, mate."

"I... I... sorry, I—" Ashton faltered, lowering his hand. Queasiness rolled through his stomach, his heart thumping erratically. "Sorry."

"No harm done." Sara smiled.

"You're Glue-Chair Lady," Violet said, peering around her brother's elbow. Sara huffed, planting her hands on her hips.

"By Seltik, is that how people are going to remember me?" She sighed, head tipping disappointedly. "So be it. I'll sue Lacey later." She smiled again. "I recognised you from the medbay, thought you looked a little lost."

"We are." Ashton admitted, swallowing dryly. He tried for a smile too, plonking a hand on Violet's head. "Know anywhere we can get a hairbrush?"

"Oh, the hairdressers. They always have spare stuff. They're only the next floor up, come, come." She waved for them to follow her.

"Please be less than a hundred and thirty-six stairs," Ashton mumbled.

Sara laughed.

"Found the Devil Stairs then?"

"Please tell me they're called Devil Stairs because they're a devil on the legs."

"Mm... Will it make you feel better if I did?"

"Not after that question."

Sara laughed again. Out of the corner of his eye, Ashton saw Violet tip her head. He didn't get to say anything, Sara turning them onto a familiar set of stairs, the very ones Finn had dragged them up.

"Floor Three belongs to the shapeshifters. Best to keep them all in one place, they like to mix with Floor Six," Sara grimaced. "But yeah, all our hairdressing, cosmetic and fashion needs... Floor Three will know what to do."

"Are all the floors organised like that?"

"Pretty much. Ground Floor or First Floor – it's a never-ending debate – is the 'welcome mat'," she stuck air quotes around it, "where we have meals and tournaments and shows and stuff. Best to experience those than explain them. Oh, and the classrooms and training rooms are down there too. Floor Two, as you saw, is all the elements. Water, earth, fire, air, plants, electricity, and so on. There's a lot to unpack there, worry about that later. Floor Three, shapeshifters. Four is psychics and soothsayers—"

"Really?"

"Yes. Five is mostly residential, storage and production and all that, but we do keep our best creators there too. They're so happy in a room full of junk. If Lacey gets on my nerves, I just lock her in one of the rooms."

"Is she in there now?"

"Yes, she glued me to a chair. Anyway, Floor Six—"

"Hates Finn." Violet supplied.

"Ah, met them already, have you?" Sara grinned slyly. Violet nodded meekly. "Seven is our obscurities. Abilities that don't fit on the other floors as well, like talking to animals or running super-fast or, uh… there's someone up there that can make glue. Just—" She flailed her hands. "He just makes glue. I don't know. Comes in handy when we're doing papier-mâché."

"I bet."

"Yeah, anyway. Eight is Michael's office, the library, game rooms and the cinema—"

"There's a cinema here?"

"Yes. And it's *free*. Like, some of us can work there if we want, but we don't have to pay anything."

"What's a cinema?" Violet asked.

Sara stared at her, eyes widening.

"Big dark room with lots of chairs where you can watch films and eat popcorn.," Ashton explained.

He looked at Sara, silently urging her to continue. It took her a second, but she shook her head.

"I think that's everything. Main stuff, anyway. Anything

I've missed comes with experience. You *are* staying, aren't you?" She smiled sweetly at Ashton.

"We are while we figure things out," he replied evenly. He jostled Violet's hand, smiling at her. "One day at a time, right, Vi?"

She nodded, tugging lightly on a lock of hair.

Sara took Ashton by the elbow, pulling the pair to the left, swinging a door open.

"Khaled!" she called in a sing-song voice. "New customers!"

Khaled was an older man, fifties or maybe sixties, no taller than five-foot-six with dark-brown skin and brown eyes so deep they appeared black. His hair and beard were thick, once black as night, now greying, neatly trimmed. He wore a tidy black shirt tucked into smart black trousers and a fresh pair of black trainers—the guy clearly knew his style. He grinned at them, eyes sparkling. He grasped Ashton's hand in both of his, pumping twice and then the same to Violet.

Sara nodded at the siblings. "Khaled doesn't talk, but he knows *exactly* how people want their hair." Khaled patted Violet's shoulder, pointing to a chair.

Ashton egged her on with a nod and a smile and she let his hand go to follow the hairdresser curiously. "Tea? Coffee?" Sara offered. "Both?" Ashton did a double take. "We have custard creams as pancake toppings. We're weird. Get used to it."

"Tea please, milk and two sugars."

"On it." She motioned for him to sit. There were red cushioned vinyl benches along the left-hand wall, broken up by coffee tables buried under magazines and crosswords, most of which were completed albeit not with the right words. The floor was black-and-white checks, the walls were white and bedecked with portraits of many, many hairstyles. The hairdresser chairs matched the benches.

Violet was in one of these now, swinging her feet and playing with the black shawl Khaled had thrown around her. The mirrors were silver framed rectangles surrounded by softly lit bulbs. Violet waved at Ashton in the reflection, and he waved back. Music played from somewhere, gentle yet upbeat, in a language Ashton couldn't place. He noticed Khaled dancing and sashaying along to it, holding an imaginary dance partner. He kicked his foot out behind him, flicking his head back too. Violet giggled, clapping with her hands moving under the shawl. Khaled spun, flourishing a hairbrush and a spray bottle of water that seemed to spring from thin air. He continued to dance and wriggle around as he dampened and brushed her hair, juggling the instruments, spinning the bottle on his fingers like a cowboy with a gun, grazing the flat of the brush across her nose if she moved or giggled, only entertaining her more.

Ashton looked down at the magazines, a cup of tea appearing under his nose.

"Here," Sara smiled, sitting beside him and nursing her own mug. "She's a sweet kid."

"Yeah."

"Your dad's a git."

"That's one word for him," he sighed, taking a tentative sip. *Perfect.* "Thanks for bringing us here. We'd have wandered around forever."

"I know, this place is a *maze*." She laughed, patting his arm. "If you ever get lost, just ask someone or use the comms. And stay away from the Devil Stairs."

"Done."

"They move."

"Hate that."

"Floor Six jinxed them to move around the place. Sometimes, they don't lead anywhere, which is fun. Sometimes you can walk down them and end up four flights up or vice versa. But," she lowered her voice to a dramatic whisper, "it's *super* haunted."

"Yaaaay…"

"Rumour has it, the stairs belonged to the building that was here before Michael's family took over. Some big, old abandoned something or other. Only the stairs survived. It's said," she dropped her volume again; Ashton had to lean forward to hear her, "that whoever owned that building summoned the Devil. And the Devil *never left*."

"So… he's latched onto the only bit that survived?"

"Yep."

"And, uh… he's still there?"

"Oh-ho-ho, yes indeedy!"

"I do love a side helping of Devil-possessed stairs in a secret mutant stronghold."

She snorted with laughter. Ashton noticed Violet was watching in the mirror, a slight frown pulling at her features. Khaled was sharpening a pair of scissors, shuffling on his feet to the music. Violet's reflection disappeared when the hairdresser moved in, snip-snip-snipping away.

Sara blew on her tea. "I think you should stay. It'll be good for Violet to be around her own kind. And you'll both be safe here."

"It's Violet's decision really. I just—"

He hesitated, sipping his tea to fill the gap. Khaled was gaping at the brush, having been brushing her hair with the paddle. He wagged a finger at it, shaking his head in reprimand. The hand holding the brush jolted and he silently screamed in mock terror, the bristles attacking his beard. Violet laughed, reaching out a hand to help him. Between them, they wrestled the wayward hairbrush onto the counter. Khaled aimed the hair dryer at it, threatening to shoot. The brush trembled and then stilled, surrendering. Khaled nodded once – *so I thought* – and high-fived his helpful customer.

Ashton filled his lungs, sighing. "She deserves a chance to be a normal kid. We've only been here a couple of days, but... I've seen her smile more here than I've seen in years back there."

"So, you'll stay?"

"Probably. Up to her though."

Sara nodded. She snapped her fingers, catching a plate of biscuits that dropped from the air. She offered it to him first. He picked a shortie, mumbling his thanks. "How long have you been here?"

"I was born here, actually. My parents were close friends with Michael's uncle, may he rest in peace. He was lovely, used to help me with my homework—my dads *suck* at maths."

She laughed again. She was completely different to the girl from before, the one cussing her chair-gluing friend out for all to hear. Ashton wasn't sure what to make of it.

He looked over to Violet. Khaled was shimmying around, still bobbing away to the music. The left side of her hair was free of tangles and cut to her shoulder. The right side was gradually getting the same shortening treatment. She waved at Ashton in the mirror again. He smiled and waved back. Khaled noticed the motion, spinning on his heels, fists impatiently on his waist and tapping his foot. He glared pointedly at Ashton until he waved at him too, his large cheery grin snapping back into place. He waggled his fingers and returned to cutting hair.

Bright ginger locks covered the floor around them, more still showering down.

Ten minutes later, Khaled was done. He had dried her hair, cleaning away the chopped locks with a wave of his hand. With a flourish, he simultaneously spun her in the chair and removed the shawl, rolling his hand in a silent 'ta-da!'

Ashton laughed, "Oh, wow." He set his tea down to applaud.

Violet smiled bashfully. Her hair had been tidily swept back from her face, in bunches that curled at the ends ever so slightly. "I almost forgot what you looked like under that wig," Ash teased lightly, rising and shaking Khaled's hand. Khaled smiled, waving his hand as if to say, 'too kind, too kind!'

Ashton helped Violet up. She turned instantly and caught sight of herself in the mirror, hands coming up to flick the new style experimentally.

"Like it?" Ashton tapped her shoulder. She nodded eagerly. "What do you say?"

"Thank you." She shook Khaled's hand too. He pinched her cheek, cooing, until Sara came along and shooed him away. He stuck his tongue out at her, bustling away only to return a minute later with a goody bag. Inside, a hairbrush, an abundance of hairbands, clips and slides and a little book handwritten and hand-drawn—*Hair for Dumb-Dumbs*. Underneath, Khaled had scrawled his signature. He passed the bag to Ashton and with it, the responsibility of keeping Violet's hair professionally tidy. He half-laughed nervously.

"No pressure then." Khaled winked at him, mischief twinkling in his eyes.

Chapter Ten

Sara walked them back to Floor Five, where Kurtis picked them up.

"Ey, looking good, Vi!" He beamed. "Take it you saw my man Khaled? Bloke's the only one I trust with my hair," he nodded wisely.

Violet nodded along too, her new pigtails bouncing. She grinned at the movement, batting them to encourage the motion. Kurtis laughed. "What about you, Ash? No new do?"

"I'm OK, thank you."

"Pfft. Khaled is the *best*. You hungry?" he laughed again. Violet's stomach had growled; she nodded meekly. "Lunch we get ourselves. Come on, I'll show you the kitchen."

Kitchen was one word for it. It was easily twice the size of their room on five-sixteen, and as mismatched as the other communal rooms. White, chrome and black appliances – at *least* three of each – broke up the counters, some marbled, some slate, some granite, with white or black or brown cupboard doors. There were four sinks, two dishwashers and a coffee machine with a Post-it note stuck to the front—*'feed me!'*, followed by a frowny face.

Tables and chairs dotted the right side of the room, and a big window gave a view of the surrounding woods and countryside. A television on the wall was showing a Russian soap opera, someone scampering from the room in tears. Only three people were in there, hooked to the programme. One of them was crying too.

Kurtis talked them through it. "We all get cupboard space. We've got designated shoppers, so give them the list of stuff you need, and they'll get it."

"I don't have money." Ashton realised, panic prickling his chest.

"No worries, mate. A lot of us don't. Michael helps out, no questions asked. We can get jobs here, but we tend to take it in turns by the season—ain't enough work here for four thousand people."

"Michael's loaded then?"

"His whole family is. Old money. He hardly touches it, uses what he makes from selling houses to people like Yachtman," he grinned. Ashton smiled uneasily. "Anyhoo, we got some basics for you both for the time being. Any allergies, just say so—"

"Can't have strawberries."

"Both of you?"

"Makes us itchy, funny tummy."

"Cool. Noted." Kurtis nodded, pursing his lips. "Ah," he said, finally spotting the soap opera trio, "come meet your neighbours."

The trio looked up as they approached. Two men, one of whom was still teary-eyed, and the other a lady. She was rather pinch-faced in an unearthly, pretty way, her eyes impossibly blue. Her dark hair was pulled back into a high ponytail. Porcelain skin, a faint line of a scar on her cheek.

"This is Kristie with a K," Kurtis supplied. The man on the left, just as pale as Kristie with hair so finely blond that it was almost white, stared at them with coal-black eyes. "This is Stefan No-Name. Um, he abandoned his surname after family drama."

Stefan No-Name arched an eyebrow.

"I'd hardly call my father hiring my sister to kill me *family drama.*"

"We all have daddy issues, get over yourself."

"My dad is lovely," the other man said. He wiped at his eyes, extending his hand to Ashton. "I am Big Tim. Bigger than Small Tim, but smaller than Large Tim."

Big Tim was easily as tall as Ashton, beefed out under his white T-shirt. He had dark skin and darker eyes, hair cropped close to his head. He smiled with a dimple in his cheek, shaking Violet's hand too.

"And this is Violet and Ashton." Kurtis spread his hands at them like a gameshow host displaying prizes. Violet's stomach made a noise again, rumbles of laughter breaking out around the table. "Yeah, let's get some food for you. You having anything, Ash?"

"Do you have chocolate spread? I really fancy choccy sandwiches."

"Ooh." Violet brightened.

"You too?" Kurtis asked.

"Yes please."

They sat with the trio to eat. Between Kurtis and Ashton, they had made enough sandwiches for everyone, and then some. The bread was cut into triangles.

They were brought up to speed on the soap opera, English subtitles popping up for their benefit at the press of a button. Big Tim, upon hearing Violet had been to see Khaled, complimented her on her hair. She blushed a little, thanking him in a quiet voice.

It was going rather well. Violet wasn't really following the show but was content to sit and pick her crusts off. She listened to the trio chatter and bicker in Russian. Kurtis seemed to have mastered zoning them out, working his way through a mountain of sandwiches, eyes glued to the screen. Ashton was trying to follow the Russian—not that he had any experience in the language, but it was fun listening to it.

The door opened behind them. Stefan No-Name glanced over automatically, back to the conversation, then did a double take. He shushed his companions. The television was flicked off. The sudden silence and lack of entertainment zoned Kurtis back in.

"I was watching that!" he protested around his mouthful, pouting childishly. Stefan pointed, a discreet little motion he kept close to his chest. Kurtis sighed, turning in seat, Stefan facepalming as his discretion was clearly ignored. "Hey, Marlon. Didn't see you at breakfast. Sup, mate?"

"Sup?" Marlon growled.

Ashton and Violet also turned at that. Whatever they were feeding the mutants here, it was working *too* well—Marlon was similar in size and shape to Garry, white skinned with close-shaved mouse-brown hair dressed in a plain T-shirt and jeans. His eyes were either blue or grey, seething with a temper Ashton found himself on the wrong side of. "There's a *human* in my kitchen—"

"*Our* kitchen." Stefan corrected. Marlon ignored him.

"—and you say 'sup'?" he snarled at Kurtis. Kurtis pressed his lips together. He met Ashton's gaze, giving a small nod.

"Ash is here as Vi's guardian." He introduced Violet with a wave. "You know the story the same as the rest of us, mate."

"They're *Yachtman's* kids!"

"Doesn't mean they're Yachtman."

"Ooh." Violet dropped her sandwich, rubbing at her eyes. "Ow."

"What's wrong?" Ashton set a hand on her shoulder. The question came from around the table.

"Ow, ow," she groaned, head bowing. Her shoulders began to shake. Ashton scooped her up, holding her to his chest.

"I'm gonna take her back to our room," he said, rising. She whimpered, hiding her face in his shoulder. Marlon was in front of him quicker than he could blink.

"You're not going anywhere." A vein was working in his temple, spitting his words from behind clenched teeth. "Your dad killed my brother."

Ice filtered into Ashton's blood. "I... I'm sorry, but—"

Marlon roared. His hand slammed into Ashton's throat, the edge of the table ramming into his lower spine. It was a miracle Ashton didn't drop Violet. Startled yells sprang up around him, the others were on their feet.

"Let him go!"

"He had nothing to do with it!"

A hand appeared on Marlon's wrist. Violet turned her head, squinting up at him. Her fingers twitched, his jumped from Ashton's throat, as if suddenly branded. Ashton inhaled sharply, Kurtis and Tim appearing to keep him upright.

"What are you doing?" Marlon demanded, battling to keep his anger while watching his hand move against his will. His fingers curled into a fist, twisting to aim at his face. Violet had let go of his wrist, now holding something in the air, palm up, fingers wrapped around something unseen. She blinked, grimace softening, then dropping into a frown.

"I'm sorry about your brother," she said, her tone firm and level, with an undertone of sympathy, "but don't take it out on mine."

Ashton stared at her, seeing her profile. A stern expression, obstinance darkening her eyes. She was staring Marlon down. The colour had drained from his face.

"Let me go."

"Say sorry."

"Let me go!"

"Say sorry!" she snapped. Marlon flinched, clamping his free hand on the forearm he could not control.

"I'm sorry! I'm sorry!" Violet dropped her hand. His arms slumped and he gasped. He trembled as he looked at her, confusion knitting his brow. She flung a finger at the door, still glowering, and he scarpered. The door banged shut behind him.

"What the—?" Kurtis marvelled. The others were staring as well.

Ashton set Violet down in her seat, crouching in front of her. She had bowed her head again, eyes squeezed shut behind her fingers.

"Vi?" he croaked, throat aching at the speech. He shook her knee. "Vi?"

"Head hurts." she complained. He shook her knee again, causing her to peek between her fingers. Bruises already dappled his neck, blues and purples. Grey blotches swirled around him, speckled with green. She closed her eyes again, pitching forward. Ashton caught her, heart pounding.

***

Michael and Finn arrived. Marlon had sought the former out, the latter there anyway to pelt his friend with lollies. Upon hearing what happened, they ported straight into Floor Five's kitchen. Ashton was sitting, cradling his unconscious sister. Stefan and Tim were tidying up, at a bit of a loss as to what they were meant to do. Kristie was standing next to Ashton, wringing a cloth out into a bowl of water and laying the damp material across Violet's forehead.

"Oh, thank Seltik." Kurtis breathed once he saw the newcomers. "I have no idea what just happened, but I am equally impressed and terrified."

"Marlon said she moved him?" Finn puzzled. "How?" Kurtis shrugged, and the medic sighed. "That doesn't *help*. No lolly for you." He brushed past Kurtis. Kristie stepped aside for him, fidgeting with her hands.

"She's really burning up, Finn. She said her head hurt." He took the cloth away, feeling her forehead and then her cheeks with the back of his hand. A feverish crimson had crept over her features, mixing with a grimace. Her breathing was shallow and laboured, a little wheezy.

"What's wrong with her?" Ashton rasped. Finn glanced up, seeing the scarf of bruises on his neck once again.

"Why do people insist on strangling you?" Ashton's expression flattened. "Right, right. Vi first. Give." He held his hands out. Ashton passed Violet over, and Finn vanished with her. A moment later, Kathy appeared.

"Again?"

"Again," he confirmed miserably, coughing.

"Well, stop it," she chided, tapping her fingers on his neck. "Honestly, what would you lot do without me? Hum for me."

He hummed three notes. "Perfect." She smiled, planting her hands on her hips. He gingerly felt his throat, finding not an ounce of pain, bruising or hoarseness.

"Thank you. Can you—?"

She grabbed his arm. The kitchen melted into a vortex of shadows, morphing suddenly into the medbay. Ashton heaved, the choccy sandwiches suddenly disagreeing with him. Kathy provided a bucket just in the nick of time.

"I hate that." He groaned, groggily resurfacing.

"*I smell vomit!*" Finn's enraged shrieking came down the room. Kathy half-turned to see him flailing his arms in protest, spluttering obscenities.

"Keep your knickers on!" she laughed.

Finn floundered, clamping his hands over his nose. Kathy got rid of the bucket and Ashton's nausea with a wave of her hand. "Better?" she asked her patient.

He nodded, was given chewing gum. Kathy smirked over her shoulder. "Better?" she called to her colleague. Finn blew a raspberry in reply, returning to his own patient.

With a nod from Kathy, Ashton rose and hurried to his sister's side. His heart dropped into his stomach—she looked worse than she did in the kitchen.

"You're in my light." Finn grumbled, shooing him two steps to the left. "What was she like before?" he asked. "Using her powers."

"She'd—she used to get nosebleeds a lot."

"Doing what?"

"Moving stuff."

"Like what?"

"Pencils."

"Ah." Finn relaxed, smiling. He hopped backwards,

spinning on his heel to open a cupboard.

Ash took Violet's hand, her fingers unnervingly warm. There was a lot of rummaging and banging in the cupboard, Finn muttering to himself. He drew back to study a bottle of what looked like glow stick fluids, shaking his head and diving back in.

He eventually emerged a couple of minutes later, kicking the cupboard shut. His arms were full of jars and bottles and pouches and clumps of tied herbs. Ashton considered it all, gaze darting from one item to another. Finn rolled his eyes. "Well, it looks mad *now*. I'm not finished yet. KATHY!"

"I am *right here!*" Kathy was two beds away, fluffing pillows. "You don't need to *yell!*" She bustled over, checking Violet for herself. Finn bounced away, dumping everything on a table. He hummed while he worked, an odd combination of the *Muppets* tune and 'Twinkle-Twinkle Little Star'.

Kathy elbowed Ashton. "Don't stare at him while he works," she advised in a mumble, "he gets self-conscious and starts stupiding."

"I do not." Finn grumbled. "But stop staring at me, Ash. You're not my type."

"*No one* is your type." Kathy interjected. "Shut up and work."

"Stop distracting me then."

"You are and always will be your own distraction."

"That's the nicest thing you've ever said to me." Finn sniffed, dramatically wiping at imaginary tears. Kathy glowered at the back of his head, the weight of it making him hunch his shoulders and meekly squeak, "Yes, ma'am."

Kathy sighed, concentrating on Violet again.

"Will she be OK?" Ashton worried.

The medic shone a light in the girl's eyes, snapped her fingers by her ears in turn, nodding when Violet flinched.

Finn came back, squishing a ball of green paste between his thumb and finger. He smeared it on her cheeks and forehead, a blob on her nose, rushing off again. Kathy began rubbing the paste in.

Violet's grimace eased just a fraction and she mumbled.

Ashton could only watch the medics. Finn would make something – a paste, a vial, a medicine, an injection – passing it to Kathy to administer. Ash had no idea what each item did, but with each one, he freaked out that little bit more—*how much stuff was needed*?

Within ten minutes, the fever broke, and her colouration normalised. Another five minutes and her breathing stabilised. At the twenty-five-minute mark, she began to stir. Finn stopped dashing back and forth, leaning over her. He raised his hand slowly and then down again, just as slowly, forefinger extended to poke her between the eyes.

"Mmph." Violet winced, waving his hand away. She squinted at them, groggy and dazed, going cross-eyed upon seeing Finn less than an inch away.

"Hi," he smiled. "Feeling better? Have a lolly."

His face disappeared, replaced with a green sweet and then Kathy's hand, smacking it away.

"You'll rot her teeth!" she reprimanded. Finn hissed at her. "Go!" she ordered, pointing with a demanding flourish. "Go and do your paperwork!"

"No! Shan't!"

"Go or I *swear* to Seltik—" Kathy stomped her foot. Finn shut his mouth, swivelling neatly and walking away with all the airs and graces of someone pretending they weren't running for their life. "Little brat." Kathy muttered. "I don't get paid enough to deal with him—remind me to talk to Michael about that."

"Ow." Violet pressed her fingers to her temples. Kathy frowned.

"Your head still hurts?"

Violet gave a minute nod. Kathy leant in, her fingertips following the child's jawline up from her chin. Violet moved her hands away and Kathy pressed her thumbs above her eyebrows, fingers above her ears. "Still hurts?"

"Yes."

"Finn!"

"Ow."

"Sorry, sweetie."

"What's going on?" Finn returned, scribbling away on a clipboard. "Ash, what did you do?"

"I didn't—"

"I'm sure you didn't." He tossed the clipboard over his shoulder, papers fluttering. It landed upside down and skew-whiff on the next bed. He nudged Kathy away with his hip, setting his hands as hers had been. "Mm. You have a funny head."

"Don't say that."

"Oh, hey, Mike. You took your time."

"You can't say she's got a funny head." Michael scolded, swatting Finn's shoulder. "It's rude."

"I'm not saying—aesthetically, her head's *fine*. The squishy part inside, not so much." Ashton scrunched his nose at him.

"Living with Dad will do that to you."

"Fair." Finn moved away, biting his thumbnail. "I may

113

need a minute." He picked up the clipboard, straightening the pages and rambling off. He stopped about ten feet away and backtracked, waving as he went past and into the office.

"Idiot." Kathy snorted.

"Hear, hear." Michael nodded. "Are you all right, Ash?"

"Yes. Thank you." Ashton managed a small smile. Michael squeezed his shoulder.

"Violet?"

"Mm?"

"Do you remember what happened?"

"Mm-mm." There was the tiniest shake of her head, the movement making her squeeze her eyes shut. Michael glanced at Ashton, gesturing with his head. Ash squished Violet's hand and followed Michael a few beds away.

"What? What is it?"

"Marlon's having a, uh… let's say a tantrum. He's scared and running his mouth off. I want to forewarn you rumours and theories are spreading."

"But—" Ashton frowned. "It's just Vi though, I… I don't know how she did that, but she's never moved more than a pencil before."

Michael nodded, though Ashton wasn't sure his words had been fully heard.

"Moving inanimate objects is one thing. All mutants have telekinesis in varying strengths. Moving people like that…" Michael winced. "It doesn't look good; I won't lie to you. Has… has Violet ever shown any control over water?"

"No. No, I don't think so."

"How often did she use her powers at Yachtman's?"

"Uh… I'd get her to practise moving stuff with me, but…" Ashton shook his head, "nothing more than that. Except for

114

the colours thing."

"So, her abilities are still undetermined."

It wasn't a question. Michael was thinking aloud. His flecked gaze cut back to Violet for a moment, who was now sitting up and taking tentative sips of water with Kathy's help. "If she shows any control over water, we're going to have a problem."

"Why?"

"Water elementals are… uncommon in their field and any that pass through undergo much training and security checks."

Ashton stared at him.

Michael tapped a finger on his chest, his poke sending spirals of warmth around Ashton's lungs. "Humans are about seventy percent water, yes? Mutants are roughly the same, there may be some slight differences depending on biology, but same kettle of fish. There are a few reasons as to why she was able to move Marlon—water is the most obvious one. It's not happened for a while, touch wood," he touched his forehead, "but it's not unheard of for water users to manipulate the water inside a person's body."

"And… if she *doesn't* have water powers?"

Michael just looked at him, expression softening into a pained look of pity. Ashton didn't like that look. "Should I hope it's water?"

Michael inclined his head, biting his lower lip.

Ashton swallowed dryly, looking to his sister. "Then I hope it's water."

Chapter Eleven

By dinnertime, Violet's headache had dwindled to a dull, manageable ache. Finn brought them dinner – chips, fish fingers and peas – sitting cross-legged on the neighbouring bed to eat a chip sandwich. Michael joined them while Ashton was bribing Violet to eat her peas.

"I don't like peas either." The newcomer smiled, sitting next to Finn, feet dangling above the floor and crossed at the ankles.

Violet stuck her tongue out at the vegetables and Michael laughed. "Feeling any better?" he asked.

She nodded, picking at her chips.

"You're not helping," Ashton sighed, rolling his eyes at him. Violet turned her head the other way, mouth firmly shut. "You heard Kathy—you've got to have your five a day."

"Bleurgh."

"Do you want me to get her something else?" Finn offered.

He disappeared in a blink, returning a moment later with a tray. The tray held three bowls, all steaming with freshly cooked vegetables.

"Sweetcorn, carrots or cauliflower?"

"Why do you have—you know what?" Ashton held his hands up. As far as he was concerned, cauliflower was for roasts, not everyday dinners, but these were mutants. "Never mind."

"Now you're getting it." Finn grinned.

He floated the tray over to Violet, who eyed it sidelong. Under her brother's glower, she picked the sweetcorn, although she did swipe a handful of chopped carrots too. Ashton sighed, shaking his head and picking up his fork.

There was a *thwap* of paper. Finn caught his clipboard, handing it to Michael.

"Wow," he marvelled, "did *you* do your *own* paperwork?"

"I don't intend to make a habit of it," Finn grumbled, biting into his sandwich.

Michael set his plate aside, laying the clipboard on his lap, continuing to eat while he read. Finn narrowed his eyes at him. "Don't get grease on my stuff," he warned.

Michael nodded once, still reading.

Ashton noticed he was staring again, distracted by the sudden concentration on Michael's face, and looked quickly away from him, seeing Violet had built a den on her plate, made of fish fingers. She was holding chips by pinching the end, making them 'walk' about her plate. They were clearly having an argument of sorts as one chip kicked the other into the ketchup and proceeded to victory dance.

"Vi."

"Mm?"

"*Eat* your food."

"OK." She pointed at the losing chip. "Not that one though. That one's an imposter." She stuck her tongue out at it.

Ashton raised an eyebrow, and she shoved the winning chip in her mouth.

"Oh, is that what it was?"

The question drew his attention back to Michael. Finn

leant toward him, reading whatever his friend was pointing at. Mouth full, he nodded. "Well, that's easily dealt with," Michael smiled. "What's this?" He pointed at something else.

Finn chewed for a moment, shifting his mouthful to his cheek.

"Bob."

"That is *not* a person."

"Meant to be a dog."

"*How?*"

"I can't draw dogs."

"You can draw the heart by memory, but you can't draw dogs?"

Finn nodded.

Michael sighed. "Why are you drawing on medical reports?"

"It needed some style."

"Right." Michael shook his head, finally noticing Ashton was watching them. "Good news—Vi will be fine. She over-exerted herself, quite common in young mutants. We can work on that, start training her if she's ready for it."

He glanced at Violet, but she was busy sacrificing more chips to the ketchup. "Bad news," he continued, "we still don't know what she did. Or why she can't remember it. Or why Finn said she's got a 'funny head'." Ashton's gaze dropped to his plate. The fish fingers did not seem so appealing now. "Not to worry." Michael smiled. "I love a good puzzle."

"Oh no." Violet sat up straighter, watching the wall. Her attention drifted along it, swept down to the floor and tracing back to her hand.

"Oh no?" Ashton prompted. "What's oh no?"

She simply pointed at the door. A split second later, it

118

swung open, crashing into the wall. A man gripped the door handle, white as a sheet, a fine layer of perspiration on his skin. His blue eyes found Michael; they were wide and terrified, caught in the shadows of his choppy, dark hair.

"Barry?" Michael rose, holding the clipboard across his chest. "What's wrong?"

"They got Leona," Barry wheezed. "Her and the others, they... they got them."

Michael blinked. Finn leant forward, peering around his friend. Barry dragged his sleeve across his face. "Paul made it back. He... he's the only one."

"Where is he?"

"Your office."

Michael frowned, dropping the clipboard on the bed. He marched forward, grabbing Barry's arm and promptly disappeared. Finn shoved the last of his sandwich in his mouth, hopping up.

"What—?" Ashton began.

"Leona runs a small group, mostly recon." Finn's eyes darkened, rubbed at his jaw. "Yachtman's got them." Ashton's stomach shrivelled. Finn touched Violet's head. "How did you know Barry was there? Can you see the colours through walls?"

"No."

"Then how did—?"

"His line."

"His line?" Finn echoed. He looked at Ashton for answers, seeing his own confusion mirrored there. "What line?"

"His line," she insisted.

"Oooh..." Finn whined, massaging his temples. "This is for Michael. Come on."

He put a hand on their shoulders. Ashton squeezed his eyes shut as they ported. His half-eaten dinner was doing the cancan in his stomach. Opening his eyes took him a few seconds too, head spinning.

"I hate that," he mumbled.

Violet's hand gripped his wrist. Ash managed a wobbly smile. "I'm OK," he assured.

Finn had left them, moving to one of the chairs by Michael's desk.

Blue-haired Paul was slumped in the seat, shaking and worryingly pale. Finn began checking him over. Paul hardly noticed him. Michael had made him a cup of tea, steaming gently before him on the table.

Barry was standing by the fire with a cup of tea of his own. Michael was leaning on the front of his desk, arms folded across his chest.

"How many?"

"Dozens," Paul croaked. "They… they were waiting for us. Place was rigged. Couldn't port or anything." His voice wavered.

"They knew you'd be there." Michael sussed.

Paul nodded listlessly, watching the steam unfurl from his tea. Michael bit his knuckles, grimacing. He rose and moved around his desk, opening drawers, scouring through them.

"Look at me," Finn requested, turning Paul's head gently with his fingers under his chin, peering closely into his eyes. He hummed, concern settling. "Shower," he ordered, "go find Kurtis."

"What about—?"

"I'll think of something." Michael announced, not looking up. "Get some food, Paul. I'll call a meeting when I've got a plan."

Paul hesitated, fingers momentarily tightening on the arms of his chair.

His shoulders slumped.

"OK." He nodded once, more a head droop really, and ported away.

"Mike, Mike, Mike!" Finn flapped his hands, dashing around the table to grab his friend's shoulders and shake him. "Mike, you have to—uh, Barry, mate, could you, uh…" Finn waggled his fingers.

Barry stuck his tongue out and vanished too. "Right, what was I doing?" Finn pouted, squinting in thought. "Oh, yeah." He brightened, returning to throttling Michael. "*Miiiike!*"

"Fiiiiiinnnnnnnn!" Michael replied, throttling him back.

"She's not water!" The medic beamed, taking his hands away to clap excitedly.

Michael narrowed his eyes, gaze cutting to Violet curiously. She sidled behind her brother, hanging on to the back of his T-shirt.

"Clarify," Michael requested.

He was looking at Ashton now, expression somehow simultaneously unreadable and pained. Ashton turned away, kneeling in front of his sister, resting his hands on her shoulders.

"Are you all right?"

"Confused." She grimaced. "Did I do something wrong?"

"No." He shook his head.

Finn hissed, smacking Michael's arm for attention.

"Lines, Mike. She said she knew Barry was there because she saw his *line*."

"Line?" Michael repeated.

He put a hand to his forehead, brow creasing. Thoughts flared into a storm in his eyes. "By Seltik, that's…that's…" He dropped his hand to his chest. "Violet? Can I talk to you?"

"No," she squeaked, trembling. Tears pooled in her eyes.

"I'll do it." Ashton squeezed her in a one-arm hug, rising carefully. "What do you mean by 'lines'?"

Michael hummed indecisively, pressing his hands together. He shot Finn a look – hesitant? Confused? – tapped his fingertips against each other and sighed.

"I don't really know," he replied.

"Come again?"

"Well… I've read about 'lines'. Or… uh…" He frowned, closing his eyes for a moment. "That's the one." He brightened, recollecting something.

He held his hand out. A book rushed past Ashton's head, startling him. It was similar to the faded black book Michael had called upon about Violet's colours, but red instead. He flicked through, Finn peering over his shoulder curiously. "Here we go," he eventually said, tapping a page past halfway. "This was my grandfather's book, passed on to my uncle, passed on to me. Grandad studied obscurities more than anything else, used to travel the world to find out what he could." He leant slightly, dislodging Finn from his shoulder, trying to see Violet, who was still hiding behind her brother.

When she didn't come out, Michael carried on. "Grandad called them 'strings'. He says he once met a mutant, living alone somewhere in the Amazon Rainforest. They were hiding. He wrote that the mutant told him that they could not cope with seeing strings cut, but not much more than that. Grandad came up with theories but had no real evidence." Michael considered the notes again. "What line did you see on

Barry?"

"Blue," Violet mumbled, shifting at Ashton's elbow. "Like the sky." Michael scratched at his chin, passing the book to Finn. The medic made a face at the notes but read quietly. "Bad." Violet hid again.

Michael held his hands up in reassurance.

"It's OK."

"No." She shook her head, hiding her face. "Yellow."

"Yellow was good, wasn't it?"

"Dark yellow."

"Ah." Michael tucked his hands in his pockets, rocking on the soles of his feet.

Finn turned a page, Michael turning his head at the noise. "Violet," he said carefully, "I'm going to ask you something. You don't have to answer me if you don't want to, I will understand. But it is still important. Is that OK?" He kept his tone light, carefully arranged.

He could see Violet, or her shoulder and wisps of her hair at least, dithering behind Ashton. For almost a minute, she remained concealed.

Michael gave a little sigh of relief when she finally poked her head out a fraction.

"What… what is it?"

"Would you help me? Help me understand these lines?"

"Bad?"

"No. I don't think so."

"Why?"

"Because if these lines are what I think they are, what Grandad thought they were, then… then maybe we could save our friends." Her eyes widened and she ducked back.

Ashton frowned at him, placing a hand on his sister's

head. "I know, I know." Michael raised his hands placatingly. "I don't want you – either of you – anywhere near Yachtman either. But we might have an advantage with you, Violet, and do what we've not done before."

She faced him again, although she kept her gaze on the floor at his feet.

"What?" she asked in a voice no louder than a whisper.

"Get back our own," Michael answered. "Will you help?"

***

Michael called the meeting twenty minutes later. He kept his grandfather's book with him, having slid an old Greggs' receipt to mark the page he needed. He had told them he would catch up. Finn led them away – Ash refused to port again, his stomach already despised him enough.

The meeting was held on the top floor, so they didn't have far to go, to a large cinema. Three hundred people could plop themselves down on cushioned, red seats staggered in tiers. The stairs were lit in strips along the edges, softly alternating in rainbow colours. There was nothing on the large screen, the lights were still up and there was quiet music playing through the speakers, maybe jazz.

Ashton was staring at a speaker, high up on the wall, contemplating throwing his shoe at it.

A tug on his hand drew his attention away from the music choice. Violet was surveying the gathering, peeking around his elbow. About twenty mutants had sprawled out in the middle rows, bickering and shoving and zapping each other with their powers.

He saw Garry with two Rs sitting with a thunderous

expression on an aisle seat, the shapeshifter next to him impersonating various politicians and poking him in the cheek. Finn bounced up the steps, Kathy waving him over, Jeevan asleep on her shoulder.

There was Ryan with the frogspawn, watching Finn with a malicious gleam in his eyes and a smirk.

Kurtis was there, his arm around Paul, who sat with his head in his hands. They sat closer to the front than the others, three rows in between. Khaled was the closest to them, studying Paul's blue hair with an unapproving eye.

Ashton didn't recognise anyone else. Mutants of various ages and forms and from many, many floors, mixed together, antagonising each other out of boredom.

A shadow fell over him and he hunched his shoulders. He could feel Marlon's glare in the back of his skull. Violet had stiffened beside him, not even daring to blink.

"Why are you here?" he snarled.

"Because I asked them to be," came Michael's voice from behind Marlon.

"But—"

"Please sit down."

"But she—"

"I know. I think I've figured it out." Michael motioned to the seats. Marlon scowled and stomped up the steps, collapsing sulkily into a seat behind the medics.

Upon seeing Michael, the shoving and quarrelling and mimicking Members of Parliament ceased within the space of a heartbeat. Michael stood still, looking up at them, the book held close to his chest. His eyes travelled over his shushed audience, eventually landing on the siblings. He nodded at Ashton, who directed Violet to a seat next to Paul, sitting on her other side.

Michael checked the crowd again, a minor crease forming between his eyebrows. "Where's Barry?"

"I thought you said Garry." Kathy frowned.

"I said Barry *and* Garry."

"Oh." Kathy scrunched her nose. "One sec." She ported. Jeevan, having lost his pillow, face-planted the back of her seat, rudely awoken and groaning loudly to make sure everyone knew.

Finn wriggled into Kathy's seat, supplying the shoulder-pillow. His colleague was asleep again in seconds.

"He reattached two legs last night, people. Give him a break."

"Whose legs?"

"You know Tina in the kitchens?"

"Yeah."

"Her cousin."

"The exploding one?"

"She only has one cousin."

"Just checking."

"Exploding cousin?" Violet whispered.

Ashton saw his own bewilderment on her pale features; he was only able to offer a shrug.

Michael sighed, cleaning his glasses on his shirt. Finn yelped as Kathy returned, landing on top of him and furious her seat had been stolen.

Barry materialised next to Ash, facing the rear of the room.

"One day I'll get it," he muttered, plonking himself next to Ashton. "Hey, Paul?" Barry called softly, leaning forward to see past the siblings. "You all right, mate?"

Paul didn't seem to hear him. Kurtis see-sawed his hand, grimacing.

Barry sat back, rubbing at his eyes.

"All right," Michael called, pushing his glasses up his nose, "that's everyone. Finn, shush. She's not going to kill you."

"Haha! Nepotism!"

"I have been awake for *eighteen hours*," Jeevan hissed stubbornly, keeping his eyes shut, "repairing the legs of a living *bomb*."

"We'll be quiet."

"Here, have a lolly."

"*Finn*," Michael and Kathy both scolded.

Finn shrunk in his seat, grumbling.

Jeevan huffed and turned to Kathy's shoulder to resume napping.

Michael shifted his hold on his book. "OK, settle down." Just as before, everyone's focus was on him, not a single noise, not even Jeevan's snoring. "As you're aware, Leona and her recon team were ambushed. Paul... Paul was the only one to get away." Michael looked at the blue-haired man, running his fingers up and down the book's spine. "I sent Brenda ahead to scout—all we know so far is that they're being held in a facility."

"They're still alive?"

"I hope so."

"Are we going to get them?" Paul's voice was hardly more than a whimper. Ashton, two seats away, hardly heard him.

Michael, with his enhanced hearing, bit the inside of his cheek, mulling something over.

"I *do* have an idea. But it's super risky. I don't want to lose some to get some. That is not a call I'm willing to make. However, I— I *think* I've got something." He turned the book over in his hands.

No one pressed him, letting him gather his thoughts. "Well…" He looked over to Violet. Marlon was on his feet in a second.

"No! She could have killed me!"

"She's the size of your little finger, mate," Finn scoffed, shaking his head. Marlon coloured furiously.

"Marlon said she moved him," the shapeshifter remarked.

"Is she water?" someone else asked.

"Please let her be water."

"She's not water." Michael flicked the cover of his book. Collective protests sprang up, the silence broken as people raged and Marlon crowed that he was right, he was right! Michael let them steam for a minute.

Violet covered her ears, doubling over in her chair, Ashton's hands quickly moving over her own. He sent a glare Michael's way, only to see the leader was already looking at him. He gave a quick motion with his fingers—*wait.*

He waited for a lull, raising an eyebrow for quiet. "She's not water," he repeated, "but she's also not what you fear. She's something new. Or, at least, new to me."

"New?" Barry echoed.

"Let's say rare. Really, really, really… really, really, really, really rare."

"Ooh, that's top level rare," Barry admired, looking aside to nod at Violet.

She was unaware, having drawn her knees to her chest, ears still covered.

"Yes, top level," Michael agreed. "Violet, is it OK if I tell them?"

When she didn't answer, he redirected the question to her brother. Ashton frowned.

Michael didn't press. "All right," he said. "We'll come to that later. There's... there *is* something I want to put to you all." Michael bit his thumbnail, studying his group of delinquents again. "Yachtman knew Leona was going to be there. Someone told him. He was ready. Now, our friends are in danger."

"A spy?"

"Yes."

"Are you sure?"

"Yes."

"Who?" Marlon demanded.

"If I knew that, I would've dealt with them by now."

"I've a pretty good idea," Marlon glowered. "We have two of his kids right *there.*"

He pointed at the duo just in case no one else had seen them.

Ashton swivelled in his seat, argument boiling on his tongue. Marlon clenched his fists, ready to shout.

"No." Michael put a finger to his lips.

Ashton's temper dropped from him, dispersing a shiver down his spine. Marlon sank back into his seat, oddly contrite. "These two are welcome guests," Michael said. "Violet was inches from death by Yachtman's hand and Ash may have fared no better. They are safe here and I do not believe they would turn us over to their sorry excuse of a father."

Ashton stared at him. Partly grateful for defending them—this man had only known them a handful of days and was prepared to stick his neck out for them.

On the other hand, he was mystified. What had Michael done? What were his abilities, to stop a fight so easily like that? Now that he thought about it, all he had been told about Michael consisted of three things—he was the big boss, he was record-breakingly clever and he was super rich from selling houses to people that hated him but had no idea who he really was.

Michael was speaking again. "There is, without a doubt, a mole. I will work to get to the bottom of it as quickly and as quietly as I can. I would appreciate if this information did not leave this room. Is that clear?"

There were murmurs of agreement and 'Yes, Michael's' and the odd nod here and there.

Violet looked up at the quieter tones, tentatively lowering her hands. She threw a curious look to her brother and then cocked her head to examine Michael. He noticed her immediately, smiling.

"How are you feeling, Vi?"

She mustered a little head wobble and his smile softened in understanding. "Meetings can be a tad daunting, but I'm not expecting you to get up and sing for us, I promise."

A quick, polite flash of a smile was all he got in response.

Paul shifted in his seat, sitting up straighter.

"Mike…"

"I'm getting there." Michael promised. "Did you eat?" Paul stared at him as if he had suddenly started speaking an alien language.

"He had toast," Kurtis filled in.

"Thank you. Violet?"

"Mm?"

"Do you mind if I tell everyone? It won't leave this room

either."

"OK."

"Yeah?"

She nodded, tucking her chin to her chest. Michael's grateful smile went unnoticed by her.

Khaled clambered his way over the seats to sit behind her, a hairbrush appearing in his hand. He tapped her on the shoulder with it, grinning broadly. He began brushing out her hair, deftly distracting her.

"OK." Michael had everyone's rapt attention. "Violet is not water; we have established as much. She is also *not* the other things we have to worry about, which is an absolute one-in-a-million chance I never could have dreamed of. From what I understand, her abilities are still developing, perhaps delayed by Yachtman's abuse. However, she and her brother here have been rather informative. Violet can see colours." There was a beat and then:

"Woo!" Barry clapped enthusiastically, the applause echoing sadly in the screen.

He did not relent until Ashton gently pushed his hands down.

"Thank you, Barry." Michael inclined his head. "But what I mean is she can see *our* colours. They are around us and vary with our mood and intentions and... etc. It's not something I've seen myself, but my uncle and grandfather made notes about it. Actually, quite fascinating, forgive me if I nerd out."

"How do mood colours—?"

"Move you?" Michael finished.

Marlon's expression was surly, nodding. Michael beamed. "They can't!" he said, clutching his book excitedly.

"Oh, Seltik, here it comes," Finn complained. "Mike, tone

131

the nerding down by, like, ninety percent."

"Mmph. I'm trying." Michael pulled a face.

He gave himself a moment, ignoring the few titters of laughter in the audience. "I'm good. Don't look at me like that, I am." He adjusted his glasses, smiling again. "Barry," he gestured to him, and Barry sat up straighter, straightening his shirt, "Vi knew you were coming to the medbay. She saw your line."

"My line?"

"Yep. Grandad called them strings. If his theories are right, Violet was quite possibly seeing your life string."

"Is that good?"

"Does it—?"

"Move you?"

"Will you—?"

"Stop that? No. No, I won't." Michael smirked, flickers of mischief dancing through his eyes. "And maybe. I'm still piecing it together. No, don't sidetrack me. If Violet is willing to help me, and it actually works, I think we would be able to track Leona and the others using their life strings."

"So, what? We could sneak in?"

"Yes. And a smaller team too, what with there being less ground to cover."

"What if we can't port out?"

"I've been studying Yachtman's facility. His security measures are mostly tech-reliable and while they block porting, we can still get through walls and floors. I'll take a couple of earth elementals with me, we'll—"

"Wait, *you're* going?" Finn frowned. Protests rose, as did most of the mutants, getting to their feet to argue.

"Easy, easy." Michael gestured for quiet. "I approved the

recon. I approved Violet and Ashton staying here. It's only fair that I go and, with Ash staying here—"

"Excuse me, since when?" Ashton countered, also standing. "She's my sister; I'm not leaving her!"

"I get that, but humans aren't very well adapted to the rockies' burrowing."

"But—"

"I will be by Violet's side the entire time, I swear to Seltik." Michael put a hand on his heart. Ashton opened his mouth, determined. Small fingers curled around his, giving a soft squish.

"Vi, no—"

"Have to."

"No—"

"Want to."

"But how—? What... what about him? What if he gets you again?" Ash sat on the edge of his seat, holding her hand in both of his. She studied his face, biting her lower lip.

"Ash," Michael called gently, "I'll keep her safe. I promise."

"She's just a kid."

"I know. But she's also got abilities we've never had here. She would make a huge difference." Michael's tone was soft, hopeful.

Ashton looked at his sister again, picking at his lip. She was watching something by his ear. Michael shifted on his heels. "My offer still stands," he said. "You are both welcome to stay here, for as long as you like. We will keep you safe from him."

Ashton stayed quiet, thoughts flurrying. He abhorred the idea of Violet going somewhere without him, *especially* to this facility.

Yes, there was a chance to rescue those captured mutants, but what risk did it bring on his sister? They had escaped and now Michael wanted to drag her into the fray. It made his stomach churn.

But there was a positive here. A couple, actually.

First and foremost, they were being offered a home, a *safe* home, where Violet could be herself, be the kid she hadn't had the chance to be, learn more about her own kind.

Secondly... he couldn't stop her from going on this mission. She had made that decision herself. As much as he didn't want to let go, she had found herself a purpose, something she didn't have before either.

"OK," he sighed. "OK."

Violet smiled at him, cautiously thankful. He put a hand on her head, returning a feeble smile. "You listen to Michael now, all right?"

She nodded. Khaled smacked his hand away with the hairbrush, silently tut-tut-tutting. Ashton mumbled an apology, nursing his bruised knuckles. "And you," Ash glared sidelong at Michael, "if anything happens to her, I'll bring it back on you tenfold. Clear?" Michael blinked, no longer smiling. He glanced over to the medics, blank confusion wrung across his face.

"Well, snap," Finn snickered, knuckles whitening excitedly on the seat in front. "The hooman's got some *nerve*." He narrowed his eyes at Michael and then flipped the squint on Ashton. "I have tried for *years* to shut him up. *You* come along and stun him speechless in *five flaming minutes*." He squinted some more, eyes practically shut. "That's pretty sus, mate." Ashton ignored him, glowering demandingly at the

134

leader.

"Mm." Michael straightened his glasses. "I understand. Violet will be under my protection."

He fiddled with the receipt in his book, humming to himself.

Finn cleared his throat, startling Michael from his thoughts. "Right, yes. Vi, can I borrow you? Ash, can you, uh, can you help Kurtis? Make sure Paul gets some rest."

"I'm coming too!" Paul protested, on his feet. Michael shot him a look, regaining enough of his composure to do so. Paul seemed to deflate, even his hair. "I'm sorry," he croaked.

"You have nothing to apologise for," Michael said firmly. "Now go to bed or you're grounded."

Chapter Twelve

Ashton refused to leave Violet's side until the mission. It was only when they were gone would he pick up his assignment in helping Kurtis with Paul. Michael didn't argue. Finn thought it was great.

"Ooh, the hooman scared you good, didn't he? Didn't he, Mike?"

"Will you *please* stop poking my face?" Michael grumbled.

Finn smirked, jabbing his finger in his friend's cheek. "I hate you."

"That's the biggest pile of bull I've heard in my life. Poke."

"You don't have to narrate your pokes."

"Poke, poke, poke."

"Um," Ashton raised his hand, "the mission? Saving your friends?"

"Yes." Michael agreed, smacking Finn's hand away. "Vi. How many strings do you see?"

"Blue ones?"

"Are… there other ones?"

She nodded, twisting a fine lock of hair that had come free at her hairline. Michael and Finn exchanged looks. "What other ones?"

Violet didn't answer, mumble-singing the *Pokémon* theme song. Michael looked most confused, quick to shake his head and save his questions for later. "Um… OK," he said. "Do you see blue ones on us?"

Another nod.

"Do you see them on anyone outside?"

Nodded again.

"How do you see it?"

"With my eyes."

"No, I mean—*no*," Michael laughed.

Violet blinked, letting go of her hair. Finn snickered next to him. At her offended look, Michael hurriedly quelled his amusement. "I mean, if you're seeing more than one, what are they like?"

"On the floor."

"Any pattern to them? Any order?"

"Mmmm… no."

"How many?"

"Lots."

"How far do they go?"

"Everywhere."

"In the building or outside?"

"Yes."

"On the grounds then?"

"Yes."

"Any further than that?"

She shook her head, going cross-eyed as the stray hair bounced, catching it in a pinch. Michael snapped his fingers. A line of photographs appeared on the desk, in tidy rows.

Ashton assumed the occupants were the kidnapped mutants. Each one showed them doing something *normal*, living their lives—at the beach with family, screaming on a rollercoaster, nursing a milkshake-induced brain freeze, with children and pets and friends, dressed up for holidays. He picked up one closer to him, a woman in her thirties; soft, brown skin, her curly hair tucked into a bonnet. She looked exhausted, but was smiling like the Cheshire Cat, cradling two newborn babies wrapped in orange blankets.

"That's Leona," Finn supplied. "The twins are only a few months old." He pulled a face. "Babies are so grubby."

"You were a baby once."

"I was someone else's problem then, not mine."

"I'm a twin." Violet remembered. "She doesn't like me though." Ashton didn't say anything to that, not out loud anyway. Violet and Daisy never really got the chance to be twins, but that was a discussion for later. He set Leona's photo down, gaze lingering on the babies.

"Vi," he said, "you can help them, right?"

"I can try." She nodded. Pride welled in his chest, and he smiled at her.

"That's my girl."

***

"I don't understand why this is so hard for you," David sighed. The mutant glared up at him, spitting blood at his feet. "I just want to know where it is." His fist slammed into its jaw again, a satisfying crack of bone.

"Leave her alone!" one of the others cried.

"Back for some more, are you?" David laughed.

This one stared up at him, one eye swollen shut, the other bloodshot. Its nose gushed from the break his boot had caused, its mouth was bleeding.

David motioned to the soldier by the door, holding his

hand out expectantly. A prod was placed in his grip, and he smiled, relishing in the zaps and buzzes of the instrument. The mutant eyed it up, fighting to suppress the terrified tremble racking its body. It moved awkwardly, ribs broken. David swung the prod, aiming it at the beast's face. "Are you going to talk then?"

It stayed quiet. David snarled, plunging the electrified end straight at its chest. A sustained lightning strike—that's how one of his scientists had described the weapon's effect. Bright, flashing bolts ricocheted across, around and through the mutant. Its screams reached new heights of pain; torn from it with all the blasting, greedy force of a relentless storm, ripping at its throat as its skin and flesh began to burn.

The others were screaming too. *"Stop it! Stop it! Please stop it!"*

He laughed again, twisting the prod in just that little bit more. The mutant thrashed, spine arching. Its head cracked on the floor as it collapsed, fitting, and choking, bloody froth staining the floor.

Coughing behind him, the cries of the others changed. *"Leona, no! No!"*

He relented then, seeing the one with the broken jaw convulsing.

"Well, that was rather stupid, wasn't it?" he remarked delightedly.

Each captive was bound by handcuffs behind their backs. They were not made of any special metal, but they would administer a unique concoction of his creation directly into their veins should they try to use their powers. It was an agonising, consuming poison that targeted mutant cells. This Leona would be dead within an hour, mangled and destroyed from inside. As she fitted, head slamming into the floor, he smiled. He was quite looking forward to seeing this.

**

Violet had gone quiet once away from her brother, which was something considerable seeing as she hardly made a noise anyway. She hovered by Michael's side, watching him describe the facility to the two rookies he had recruited— Large Tim (not the Tim she had met before, that was Big Tim) and Rhonda. Large Tim looked like he ate Garrys with two Rs for breakfast, he towered over them all—Michael came to his elbow. Violet wasn't sure what his face looked like, but he was tan and dressed all in black. His hair was either brown or dark-brown, it was hard to tell with it being all the way up there.

Rhonda was tall too, though not as tall as Large Tim, just a little taller than Michael. She had light-blonde hair pulled back in a bun, stony brown eyes, a strong jaw and a warm smile as she introduced herself to Violet with a firm, calloused handshake.

This woman may not have eaten Garrys for breakfast, but she certainly had the next thing down, the muscles of one arm probably weighing as much as Violet did.

"Aww, you've got an admirer." Finn grinned at Rhonda. He had refused to go, even though he wasn't on the mission, eating from a large jar of cookies and getting crumbs all down his front and chocolate on his face. "I named them," he told Violet, smirking proudly, gesturing at the elementals. "Rockies, splashers, burners, hairdryers, zappers and leafies."

Violet stared at him. "No one likes the names," he shrugged, "but we use them anyway." He grinned mischievously, offering her the jar.

She glanced at Michael – he had already protested that it was his secret stash – but he nodded at her, so she took one, mumbling her thanks.

She sniffed it first, smelling chocolate and butter and sugar. Food smelt different here. A nicer different.

Michael began explaining the plan and she stationed herself next to him, nibbling on the biscuit.

The photographs were on the table. Michael hoped that seeing their faces would help her see their strings.

So far, all she could see were the ones in the room. She could see others too, outside the room, but they were hazy and faded with distance, hundreds upon hundreds of them humming and weaving and jumping as their owners moved around. It was a little nauseating to watch them, it needed some getting used to. She hadn't seen the strings before coming here.

Blinking, she thought of the other strings that had popped up. Red and yellow ones.

Unlike the blue ones, which were all different lengths and seemed to trail behind the person, the reds connected people in pairs or threes, even a couple of fours, growing and shrinking in length and never weakening, no matter how far apart the people were.

She had also seen red strings that wriggled around, only attached to one person, searching for something. Some stretched as far as she could see, beyond the grounds. And some people didn't have one.

Yellow strings were more confusing. They varied greatly in saturation and condition and lengths. A lot of the ones she saw were dull, cut and dragging on the floor. Some ebbed with feeble light, fraying like old twine.

She had only seen one in perfect condition—Michael's. It seemed to glow, so bright in colour it was, not a single strand out of place. It wasn't solidly connected to anything, like red ones, but danced around him in spirals and loops and waves.

She wasn't sure how she knew, but she *knew* that the string was home here in this place and thrived because of it.

She hadn't told Michael about those ones. Didn't want to, not yet. All of this string business, she wanted to get more accustomed to it, before giving him more information. She could tell he wanted to know though. His colour was more yellow than before, like super-concentrated sunflowers; he was frantic to know more about her ability. Excited didn't cover it.

Her attention fell to the photographs, the one with the lady holding her newborn twins. She was a happy, proud lady, teeming with love for her babies. Violet's fingertips traced the line of her face. Her arm jerked, jarring her elbow.

"Vi?" Michael touched her hand. "Are you all right?"

She didn't hear him, rubbing her elbow. Her focus remained on the photo, the smile of a bone-tired new mother beginning to niggle at the edges of her mind.

She blinked, opening her eyes to Leona's face, no longer smiling, no longer in the picture, but in a room, with others, screaming, contorted with agony beyond measures, hands restricted behind her back.

Laughing echoed around her. Ice stabbed into her bones.

"No!" She clamped her hands over her ears, squeezing her eyes shut tight.

The laughs and the screams melded together, pinwheeling around her mind with unbridled ferocity. Bursts of colours flooded across the black expanse of her vision, iridescent and incessant.

"Violet!" A hand on her head, the colours exploded like fireworks. Michael's office returned, but at a funny angle. It took her a few seconds to understand she was lying on the floor, shivering and burning up simultaneously.

Finn was leaning over her, his hand still on her head. "Easy, easy," he reassured her.

His nose was bleeding.

She stared at the crimson trail, touching her face to see the same mess on her fingers.

"What happened?" Michael's head appeared next to Finn's, concern pulling at his features. "You were shouting. 'Stop it, stop it'."

"Stop what?" Rhonda asked.

Violet couldn't see her, somewhere to her right.

"Leona," she croaked. "He's... he's there, he's—"

Their expressions darkened. Finn helped her sit up, wiping his nose on the back of his hand.

"Easy now," he repeated.

Michael gave them each a tissue. She dabbed at her nose gingerly, dark spots flitting across her sight.

"What do we do?" she asked, watching the back of Michael's head.

Finn was checking her over for injuries. "How did I—?" Her voice broke and she squashed the tissue to her nose.

It wasn't until Finn took her hand, rubbing his thumb over the back of her knuckles, that she realised her hands were shaking.

"Nosebleeds happen when we do too much." he said kindly. "You just need some rest."

"But he said—"

143

"Don't listen to him, he's a bas—" Finn winced, floundering for a child-friendly alternative as the rockies and Michael glared at him to shush. "Uuuuhhhh… Michael! How *did* she… do that?" He circled a finger at her.

"I think…" Michael looked from his friend to his charge. "I think you somehow managed to tap into Leona's life string." He rubbed at his forehead. "OK, we've got less time than I thought. How is she, Finn?"

"She's, uh…"

"I'm OK," Violet insisted, shifting into a crouch to stand. A coppery taste had stained her tongue, the beginning of a headache pulsing between her eyes. Nosebleeds weren't a bad thing. Finn got them too. He said there was a reason, said there was a remedy. Nosebleeds *weren't* a bad thing.

Finn didn't answer Michael straight away, his expression carefully composed, though a silent objection sat in his eyes. He stayed kneeling on the floor, holding her elbow as she swayed.

A warm, gentle buzzing seeped through her from his touch, the pulsing headache winding down to a little poking. The medic looked up at Michael, holding his gaze for a moment, then reconsidering Violet.

She stared back at him, still tending her bloody nose. He shrugged.

"If she says she's OK, she's OK."

"OK." Michael waved his hand, summoning the hastily discarded cookie jar. "Eat, both of you. We leave in five minutes."

***

"If you don't stop tapping, I'm gluing you to the floor." Kurtis bonked him on the head, lightly for him, but Ashton's head was still human under the playful mutant bump.

"Ow," he deadpanned.

Kurtis smiled sheepishly. They were in his room, smaller than five-sixteen by half, but just as nicely furnished in black, white and navy. It was clear Kurtis had made himself right at home, tacking posters of bands and films on every available wall space. Clothes recently washed and neatly folded but never having made it to the drawers were piled on the desk, at the foot of the bed or on top of the chest of drawers—close enough, apparently.

Piles of books, CDs, games – both board and video – and DVDs scattered all around the room, too much for the lone shelving unit. The bed was currently occupied, Paul curled up under the *Star Trek* duvet, hugging a large floppy soft dog toy. He was asleep, but restlessly so, twitching and mumbling, clinging to the dog as though his world would vanish without it.

"Dammit," Kurtis sighed, "I'm never gonna get Mrs Hugglebun back." He pouted, looking to Ashton as if he had a solution.

When his guest stayed quiet, he scrunched his nose. "Best not to wake him."

He swung the chair around from his desk, sitting on it backwards. Ashton had dibbed the beanbag in the room – mutants loved beanbags – deciding this would be his place to sulk.

Obviously, Michael had paired him up with Kurtis to give him something to do. However, their charge didn't need them at present, and he was bouncing his knee, much to Kurtis' chagrin. Arms folded, hugging his elbows, staring out the window, knee a-bounce-bounce-bouncing, he had nothing to do.

Kurtis tipped his head. "She'll be OK. Michael will look after her."

"Not Michael I'm worried about."

"Your dad?"

"Don't call him that."

"Sorry." Kurtis bit his lower lip, eyes darting to Paul as he groaned. "Want to talk about it?"

"No," Ashton retorted a little too sharply. And then: "This sucks. I got her away from him and now she's going back. I want them to save the others, I do. I've heard too many stories about what he's done to you all, I can't—I can't imagine being on your side." He shook his head. "But I just... I'm not comfortable with—with her going." He shivered, wiped at his face. "I'm sorry. For everything."

"It's not your fault, mate."

"I'm still sorry. I hate him."

"You're not alone there." Kurtis gave a small laugh. Ashton swapped bouncing knees, ignoring Kurtis' irate stare. "You think you'll stay?"

"I hope so. Vi's been... happy here. And she can get the help she needs to understand this... string thing?" He rolled his hands.

The lines, the strings, whatever she wanted to call them— where had they come from? The colours he had always known about, but she had never used them to locate people. "What— ?" He shifted nervously on the beanbag. "Michael said you all get, uh... I can't remember what he called them, but like a set of abilities you all share."

"Inborn or primary," Kurtis supplied. "That's the porting, the summoning stuff," he snapped his fingers, catching a plate of cupcakes, "stronger, better senses, better reflexes, better looking, yada, yada, yada." He smiled lopsidedly, posing and winking as Ash stared at him, unimpressed. "Vi can learn a lot here. Not like she'll be short on teachers, now, is it?"

Ashton smiled weakly at the attempt to bolster his spirits. Kurtis offered a cupcake. "No strawberries."

"Thank you." Ashton took a chocolate one with swirly blue buttercream icing on top, bedecked with hundreds and thousands. "What about this other stuff? Michael said strings were new to him, but what about the colours? Anyone else here that can do that?"

Kurtis shook his head, biting into his cupcake and smearing icing across his cheeks and tip of his nose.

Ashton sighed, peeling the case from his treat. "Do you mind... do you mind if I ask what you can do?"

"Look absolutely radiant with half a cupcake up my nose." Kurtis struck a pose, smoothing a hand over his cornrows and winking.

Ashton was still not impressed. He pouted and bit down on more cupcake.

Kurtis smiled. "I'm a combat class," he said, "I'm quick with weapons, can use almost anything without training. Don't ask me how, Mike just said my brain's wired for it. I'm good in a scrap, let's leave it at that."

"You... don't like it?"

"My best friend re-enacted *The Day of the Triffids* while I waved a glorified stick and yelled loudly. You can laugh, fine," he turned his nose up when Ash snorted, "but when we crack out the Nerf guns, I'm coming for you first."

147

"I'm sorry."

"Too late." Kurtis helped himself to another cupcake, crumpling the wrapper and bouncing it off Ashton's temple. "Git," he grumbled.

Paul muttered something unintelligible, Kurtis' head snapping round to listen. "Trust Michael," he urged softly. "Michael knows what he's doing. He'll do right by all of us."

Ashton flicked his attention between the cupcake-inhaler and the blue-haired Mrs Hugglebun stealer.

Kurtis noticed in his peripheral vision, taking another large bite.

"Do *you* want to talk about it?" Ashton quizzed.

Kurtis shook his head, working his way through his mouthful. He was focused on his cake, the look in his eyes encouraging Ashton to change the subject. "How long have you lived here?"

"Six, maybe seven years. I forget."

"Happy?"

"And safe." He nodded. "I know it's not up to me, but I think you two should stay. Heck, even just *living* in close proximity to other mutants will make Violet stronger. We're like batteries for each other."

"So... if I duct taped about a hundred mutants together—?"

"I would not recommend it, but yes, I reckon that would cause a fair bit of mayhem."

"Have you got any duct tape?"

"No."

"You could get some." Ashton snapped his fingers to demonstrate. Kurtis threw another cupcake case ball at him. "Finn would help me."

"Until Kathy comes along."

148

"Oh, yeah, good point." Ashton hummed. Kurtis narrowed his eyes at him suspiciously. "What? I'm not plotting anything. Go away."

"This is *my* room. You go away."

"No, there's cake here." He swiped another cupcake before Kurtis could take the plate away. "Do you know anything about the Devil Stairs?"

"*Dude*, I have *so* many stories."

Chapter Thirteen

Michael drove. Violet was allowed to sit shotgun, using the visor mirror to tuck her hair into a black knit hat. It had been getting dark when they left, now night-time.

The streetlights glistened on the damp road, whisking past her in blurry trails of soft light. She cracked her window open, listening to the tires rolling on the wet tarmac, a sliver of cool night air brushing across her forehead.

"Sit back, Vi," Michael instructed kindly.

She nodded, obeyed but not taking her eyes from the outside world. "How are you feeling?"

"There's no stars."

"Mm. It's too bright around here. It's called light pollution. The stars are there, we just can't see them." He glanced at her for a moment, flicking the windscreen wipers on, raindrops splattering on the glass. "Do you see any lines?"

"Lots," she confirmed. People in cars, people on the street, people in their homes and offices. Blue, red and yellow.

"What about the colours?"

"Some."

"Can you only see them if you see the person?"

"Yes."

She scratched her head, wriggling her fingers under her new headwear. "Hat?"

"Your hair, as lovely as it is, is very noticeable. You can take it off when we're done." Michael flicked the indicator on, turning left. "You two OK back there?"

He glanced in the rear-view mirror, Rhonda and Large Tim sitting quite comfortably on the back seat. Michael had done some magic and rather than squashing the rockies in a space suitable for half of one of them, the interior had expanded to accommodate them with no changes to the outside of the vehicle.

"How far away are we?" Large Tim asked.

"I'll park up in a few. We've got some walking to do."

"Why the car though?"

"We port within twenty miles of this place, we'll have the AMCD breathing down our necks. Driving gets us close, undetected."

"Kid." Rhonda was busy tucking her hair into a hat like Violet's, leaning forward a little to address her. "You see anything yet? Leona? The others?"

"Uh…"

Violet considered the window again, no longer looking at the passing street, but the vast tangle of blue strings.

She closed her eyes, picturing Leona's proud mama face. She thought of the earlier connection, stomach twisting as the screams reverberated in her ears. "She's sick," she mumbled, hot needles prickling in her wrists. She looked at Michael, seeing grey blend with his yellow. "Bad medicine," she said. "He used bad medicine."

Her gaze dropped to her hands, palms up, fingers loosely curled around a blue string. There was no weight to it, a faint tickle of warmth on her skin.

Something was wrong with it. Despite it being the closest to her, despite her touching it, it was faded, fraying. Tightness hit her chest. "It's going away."

151

"What is?"

"Leona's line. It's going away."

"Michael…" Tim's voice hardly reached over the back seat.

Michael clenched his jaw, the car jolting as he put his foot down. A horn blared.

Violet clamped her hands over her ears, the sound rattling its way into her skull and squiggling sharply through her brain. Leona's blue line swayed in her peripheral vision, dangling from her fingers, weighted like a thought beside her head when she closed her eyes.

She opened her eyes when the car stopped, Rhonda opening the door for her. Her expression was grim, raindrops glittering across her shoulders.

She held out her hand and Violet took it, the rockie's strong fingers kindly on her own. Michael was in front, donning a black raincoat. He flicked the hood up, looking back at them.

"Ready?" Three nods. "Vi, how's Leona doing?"

She looked down at her hand, the string woven between her fingers.

"Bad."

She clenched her fist; she was going to hold onto this string, for forever if she had to. Those babies needed their mama.

Michael began walking, encased in his cloud of yellow, blue and grey. Rhonda tugged Violet forward, Tim two steps behind them, both surrounded by grey and green splotches, black pinpricks spoiling the colours.

Rain splashed on her nose; she quickly dashed it away. The weather was worsening, cold and biting. They were rather damp, merging on soaked through, within minutes.

"Not much further," Michael mumbled, pulling his hood down a little more.

They rounded the corner. Violet hiccupped a breath, tucking her chin to her chest.

Two AMCD guards stood on a doorstep, an unassuming high-end house with stone lions flanking the grey stone steps. The guards were stationed on either side of a newly painted black door.

Violet. Michael's voice materialised in her head, making her jump. He wasn't looking at her, still walking, watching his feet. *Can you see what colours they are?* He paused for a moment; Violet wondered if he could hear the questions buzzing around her mind. *I can hear some. Just think of the words, we can all hear you.*

Black. She cast a look at the men as they passed, lifting her coat collar to her nose. *Brown-black. They don't want us here.*

Ditto. Rhonda glowered.

What do we do? Tim asked, footfall half as heavy before. Violet glanced over her shoulder, seeing the green smothering the grey, the black dots browning as he glared in the guards' direction.

She looked at the string in her hand, closing her eyes to concentrate. Rhonda's grip tightened on her hand, making sure she didn't stray. She could see Leona's face in her mind again, flashing between the photograph and the poison like a flipbook. The effect niggled at the front of her brain, causing a blunt ache behind her eyes, pressing up to her forehead.

Pushing the images aside, she focused on the string. It was connected to Leona, she could see it trailing away, looping and curling and draping over the floor. It was not direct; it would take too much time—time Leona didn't have. The fraying was getting worse. The blue glow was becoming white.

Giving it a little shake, she willed it to make a beeline for its owner. The string snapped away from its hanging spots, pulling itself taut, spooling the extra in her palm and around her wrist. It hovered in the air, like a tightrope at waist height, a blue-white line stretching ahead about ten feet and then taking a left at a right angle.

There's a gap, she silently voiced. Michael glanced over his shoulder, and she pointed, hand close to her chest. *Between the buildings, there's a gap.*

Secret passage? Tim asked.

Rear access, Rhonda corrected. She held her hand out, palm down. *There's a space up ahead. Turn left... now.*

Michael snapped his fingers and the garden gate swung noiselessly open. He adjusted his hood, bowing his head, stepping into a neighbour's garden. The others followed, not a sound between them.

Another snap and the access gate opened too. Tim closed it behind them, clicking the padlock shut. It was darker down here, a damp chill prickling their wet clothes. It was a brief respite from the drizzle.

They had no interest in the neatly manicured grass or the plants trussed up in insulation for the colder months, the greenhouse pattering with rain or the pond burbling at the back. Michael focused on the stone wall to the left of the access, staring up at the top, twelve feet above at least.

OK, rockies. Your turn.

I really wish you wouldn't call us that, Rhonda mentally grumbled.

She shifted Violet's hand to Michael's, who also tucked his arm around her. Then she and Tim planted themselves on either side of them, laying a hand on their shoulders.

Almost instantly, Violet felt different. Lighter, but in the sense that someone had replaced her bones with dust. She swayed, head drooping, suddenly too heavy for her neck, staring at legs that didn't feel attached to the rest of her. Now that she thought about it, *none* of her body felt like it belonged to her, drifting in the space she had been.

She could not move as her feet sank into the grass, not disturbing a single blade. She could see the others sinking in her peripheral vision. Up to her knees in the earth now, still going.

She remembered Michael was holding onto her. She could not feel the weight of his hand on hers, but she could see his strings dancing to her right. The yellow one did not seem so bright now, even in the dark, but there was no damage to it.

The ground closed around her waist and her brain caught up. Hot needles bristled between her ribs, her breath hitching in her throat.

She clung to Leona's string, squeezing her eyes shut. Pins and needles formed in her feet, creeping their way up her lower legs.

It's all right. Michael's voice came, steady and calm. The sinking had slowed. She didn't think it was the rockies' doing. *I will get you back to your brother,* he reminded her, *I've got you.*

Her fingers twitched. His grip momentarily tightened, and the sinking found its original pace. Within seconds, the ground enveloped her head. Darkness blanketed her, she could not discern whether her eyes were open or not. Not until she

155

looked down at Leona's string.

The needles troubling at her chest swelled, burning with a new intensity, casting a blaze across her lungs, so hot it was cold.

How long they sank, she could not tell. She could still breathe, she found, like she had become a fish and her water was the rock and earth around them. She zeroed her concentration on her captive string, keeping the proud mama image in her head and not the screaming throes that had barged in.

Her feet touched solid ground. A dim light stirred beyond her eyelids. *Violet*. Michael shook her shoulder.

She opened one eye, then the other, giving a quiet sigh of relief. Michael smiled at her, nodding once. *Which way?*

They stood in a tunnel, their light coming from wall lamps with dirty bulbs. The rock walls were roughly hewn, manmade, breaking off into a series of more tunnels.

Leona's string took them back on themselves; they took the second right. Violet pointed them along, Tim now in the lead, Rhonda behind.

Michael never let go of her hand. *Any lines?* he asked. Violet tucked Leona's string to her chest, taking a breath as she considered the sprawl of strings ahead of her.

Three soldiers. She deciphered, gaze shifting across the trio of strings in question. Human, she could see them, a fuzzy image coming gradually into focus at the forefront of her mind. They were armoured up, around the next corner; a little way down the next tunnel, she could see them outside a reinforced door built into the stone wall. *Two outside, one inside.* The other lines belonged to the captured mutants.

She unfurled her last two fingers, a second string rising

and resting across the digit. *There's Imran,* she informed them, the name popping into her head. *He's hurt.*

Bad medicine? Tim worried, the grey around him spreading over the other colours.

No. Imran's string did not feel like Leona's.

A flash in the corner of her periphery, a sharp pain zipping across her temple, twitching her eye. *He's in there.* Her feet stopped moving, drawing the group to a stop.

Imran's string flashed, a single picture bursting into her thoughts. David. Bringing his boot down. Lava flooded her face, eyes watering. She put her hand over her nose, but it was not her pain. She looked up at Michael, the hot-cold needling sinking into her lungs. *He's in there.*

OK. Plan B then. He said the last bit to the rockies.

Violet didn't get to ask what 'Plan B' was. Michael closed his eyes, pressing a hand to his forehead. Rhonda reached forward, her strong hands covering Violet's ears.

Six seconds passed. A wail echoed down the tunnels, muffled by Rhonda's hands; a tinny, reverberating electronic wailing siren, accompanied by surges of red lights.

The three solider strings were moving, splitting from the main bundle. She watched the blue lines arch upwards, stretching to higher levels.

Is he still there? Michael asked, unmoving. Violet nodded.

He bit his lip, forehead creasing. The wailing racket gained a new tempo— short, sharp spatters, one long wail, three spatters, another long one, then repeat. Violet was glad for Rhonda's input, the noise incessant but manageable under her hands.

David's string began to move. Michael opened his eyes, lowering his hand. He looked questioningly at her.

He's going, she said. *After the others.* She met his gaze. *What did you do?*

I called a friend. Let's go.

They did not use the door. Michael theorised it would be rigged somehow, could call Yachtman and his soldiers back. Tim and Rhonda had no issue with this, simply sinking them through the stone walls, only fractionally less suffocating than the ground.

The moment they emerged; Violet's knees buckled. Her head swam, the room snowed under colours too extensive to pinpoint.

Her palms scraped on the rough floor; she still held the two strings. These colours wanted her attention. Their owners couldn't see who they were. It was dark in here, darker than the earth that had swallowed them, making the colours all that much brighter and demanding.

Someone was talking, to her, to the rockies, to Michael, to the others—she didn't know. She clutched the strings in both hands, tight to her chest, heart pounding beneath her fingers.

The alarm outside still screeched and spattered and screeched. The walls softened it more than Rhonda's hands, leaving space for the colours.

Green sounded like a child's cries. Black was gentle, incoherent whispers. White was murmured tones from another room. Brown laughed, malicious and revelling in it, a laugh she knew all too well.

Purples swirled across her vision, faint wisps she could hardly see. The colour deepened, blotting, quiet but present. It brought with it soft spring warmth, settling across her mind, blanketing the others, relieving and tender. She looked up, breathing raspy and wobbling.

The rockies were checking Leona and Imran over. Leona didn't have long. She was slumped on the floor, bloody sick on her chin, in a puddle near her head. A sheen of sweat on her face, glistening in the light.

Wait... What light?

Violet sat up, resting her hands on her knees for support. Michael was crouched beside her, putting a hand on her shoulder. She didn't look at him, attention trapped on her hands.

The light came from *her*. A pale-purple glow, nestling just below her skin. It pushed back the shadows, illuminating the weary, terrified, pained faces of the captured mutants.

Leona's body jerked, pulling Violet's mind back to her. The string burned warningly around her fingers; her fists clenched. There were twins, back at the Haven, twins that needed their mother. Twins that *would* get their mother.

The purple light shifted, not visibly, but stirring in her stomach and rising, like a giggle she had to keep back. Leona needed Finn. Finn could help her. In the medbay. Kathy and Jeevan too. Leona wasn't going to die. Not today.

Chapter Fourteen

Kurtis looked up, the light flickering. Ashton didn't think much of it, only looking up when it flickered again. He and Kurtis watched the light together, the latter springing to his feet at the third lapse. Ashton stared to ask, falling quiet when the light shut off. There was yelling outside, panicked and confused. Garry's booming tones thundered down the hall.

"It's a bit of dark, calm down!" he fumed.

They could hear him opening doors, checking on occupants, most of which sounded rudely awoken, going by the swearing and the challenges of 'fight me'!

Garry got to them, a tennis-ball-sized orb hovering over his palm, exuding a soft-yellow glow. "You lot all right?"

"What's going on?"

"Whole building's out. The zappers are working on it, shouldn't be—"

The light in his hand pulsed. He stared at it, a dark spot appearing in its centre. A heartbeat, then two. He shot the boys a wide-eyed look of bewilderment. Lilac hues folded out from the centre, swirling like paint in water, absorbing the yellow. Garry started and threw the ball away, cursing loudly. The ball struck the floor, bursting like a water balloon. The purple light rippled out on a wave of cool air. Screams outside, it was still going.

"Stay here!" Garry shouted, porting.

"Ugh, what was that?"

"Paul!" Kurtis exclaimed, all but throwing himself across the room.

He landed on top of his friend, hugging him so fiercely that he was choking for air in seconds. Ashton didn't interrupt, Kurtis fussing and clucking, checking Paul over, telling him how worried he was, what had just happened. Understanding dawned on the blue-haired man.

"Oh," he said, gently pushing Kurtis' shoulders for a little breathing room. "I felt it."

"You... felt it?"

"Didn't you?" Paul picked at his lip. He finally noticed their company. "Mate, that was your sister. She's back."

A beat, then...

"Ash, wait!" Kurtis cried.

Ashton did nothing of the sort, almost yanking the door from its hinges and charging into the dark hallway. He crashed into countless people instantly – *Hey, watch it! That was my foot! Manners!* – making it to the stairs with only a few bumps and bruises.

"Ash!"

He heard feet thumping on the stairs behind him, hands grabbed his shoulders. The stairwell vanished under his feet, and he toppled forward, Kurtis hauled along with him. They landed in a heap on the medbay floor, an 'oof' and a flash of blue hair, adding Paul to the pile.

"What the—?" Michael's shoes appeared, muddied trainers. "Get off him; what are you doing?"

He helped them up, one by one, Ashton winded. Michael, still dripping with rainwater, glasses steaming in the warm medbay, held him up by the elbow, his other hand feeling his ribs. "Mm, nothing broken."

"Where's Vi?"

"Ah."

Michael moved to the side, tugging Ash with him. The medbay was in complete disarray. The captured mutants were home, sprawled on the beds, filthy with grime and dried blood, more wounds than skin.

Finn and Kathy were dashing around a dark-skinned woman who was fitting and choking. Finn waved his hand, Kathy rolled her onto her side. Jeevan was three beds away, healing the jaw of a man lost under cotton bandages stained with salve and droplets of blood.

There were other medics tending to other patients, swamped with bandages and medicines and sparks of healing magic. A burst of ginger hair on a white pillow—

"Vi!" Ashton surged forward, Michael's hand falling away from his elbow. The medic caring for her took one look at him and stepped aside.

He touched her face, once more aglow with fever. "Vi?" he called. She was asleep, with a slight frown, strands of hair sticking to the perspiration on her forehead. "What happened?" There was a *click,* and the lights came back on. Cheering outside. In here, no one batted an eye, too busy, too hurt.

His eyes found the medic, dark hair already lined with grey, pale-green eyes examining him. "What happened?" Ashton repeated, voice rasping. The medic bit his lip, looking past Ashton.

"Ash?" Michael tapped his shoulder.

Ashton rounded on him instantly, a maelstrom of heat tossing his temper sky-high.

"What did you do?" he raged, grabbing a fistful of

Michael's rain-soaked coat.

"No!" Kurtis pulled on Ashton's arm, freezing when Michael raised his hand.

He recounted the mission calmly, Rhonda appearing to verify. Large Tim nodded along, but it seemed he didn't want to get too close to Violet.

"Violet got all of us out, of her own volition," Michael finished.

Ashton blinked back tears, trembling. "She did this," Michael continued gently, "I had no idea she would, no idea she *could*, but…"

He hesitated, exchanging looks with the rockies.

"But what?" Ashton demanded, jerking on the coat he still held. "But *what*?"

"Well, I had no idea she could glow purple either."

"What?" Ashton's grip slackened.

Michael kindly pried his fingers off, holding the shaking hand between his own. "What—?" Ash swallowed dryly. "I don't—"

"I've known mutants to generate their own light thousands of times before, in various ways. I have *not* seen someone light up like a glow stick before."

"Is that… bad?"

"Don't know. Don't think so. There is, um…" Michael winced. "Purple is, uh… it's not a good colour. For us." Ashton stared at him, jaw bunching demandingly. "I'll explain properly later, when things have calmed down."

He squeezed Ashton's hand, making him jump – he had forgotten about that – and let go. "Stay with your sister. I'll find you both later."

The medic had drawn up a chair, patiently standing behind

it. Ashton sank into it, the medic patting his shoulder briefly before bustling off.

"If you are not injured or a med, please leave!" Finn shouted. "I tolerate you all dearly, but you are in the way!"

"Use the comms if you need us." Kurtis smiled feebly, touching Ash's arm reassuringly.

His sideways glance at Violet did not go unnoticed. Ashton nodded numbly. Kurtis and Paul disappeared.

"Imran's clear!" Jeevan announced, turning to the neighbouring bed. "How's Leona?"

Ashton looked over his shoulder at the name, recognising her with a jolt. Her eyes were bloodshot and wide as her mouth gaped in a silent scream, a sickly pallor greying her skin.

"Fits have stopped," Kathy relayed, hastily wiping her brow.

While that sounded like good news, her tone implied that that was the easiest thing to solve.

Ash was not an expert on his father's work, but he was aware of the serum. He thought it was the worst thing David had come up with—an immediate punishment for his imprisoned mutants being themselves, using their powers. They had an hour, tops, of indescribable, excruciating agony, their body destroying itself from within. And David *loved* to watch.

Finn and Kathy did not leave Leona's side. Jeevan and the other medics dashed from patient to patient, throwing supplies and advice and updates to each other on demand.

Ashton remained with Violet, scooting his chair as close to the wall and the bed as he could. Why Finn had sent the others away, but not him, he couldn't say for sure. He wouldn't go if asked, however, but he would not hinder them either.

164

They had enough on their plates.

Violet slept through all the chaos. One of the medics gave Ash a bowl of cold water and a cloth, left him to cool her face down. She was still rather pink, but her breathing had eased by sun-up.

He kept an eye out for it, but there was no sign of this glow stick ability. Admittedly, he was rather curious—*what did it look like?* And why was purple bad for mutants? Were they allergic to purple? Michael had a purple beanbag in his pile. And he was sure he had seen mutants wearing purple, so what was it? He thought about asking Michael each time he dashed past, handing out snacks and water, but now was not the time. It could hold.

It was breakfast when Finn collapsed into a chair, cheers and applause going up. Kathy elected to lie down on the floor, groaning and short of breath.

Some of the patients had been discharged, but stubbornly stayed, awaiting the outcome of their leader. They clapped and whooped and shouted their thanks, Leona frowning at them all groggily, hands half-raised in confused defence.

Michael grinned, supplying her with water, steadying her hands as she drank.

"What happened?" she croaked, blinking back tears. "How are we—?"

"I'll explain everything later," Michael promised. "How are you feeling?"

"I'm… I'm OK. Thank you."

"I'm not," Finn chimed in, head lolling over the back of his seat. Kathy groaned in agreement. "Jee?" Finn called, closing his eyes. Jeevan rolled his eyes.

"I'm not doing your paperwork."

"No lollies for you."

"Shame." Jeevan mock-pouted, finally reaching Violet's bedside. "How are you holding up?"

He smiled warmly at Ashton.

"You guys are amazing."

"If he thanks God again, smack him for me."

"Go to sleep, Finn." Jeevan ordered light-heartedly. His colleagues were both out before he even finished his sentence, too tired to register the madness around them; too tired to pay any attention to ticking clock noises; too tired to do anything more than snore. "They'll be fine." Jeevan shook his head, holding Violet's wrist and taking her pulse.

"Did she—?"

"Overexert? Yep. She'll be fine. Finn kept some of the remedies from last time, but it's not as bad this time. It's a shock to the system the first time, the second time it's more of a... *again? Really?*" He blew a raspberry.

Ashton nodded vaguely.

Jeevan tipped his head, eyes roving Ash's face. "Your sister saved a lot of lives. Be proud."

"I am. Doesn't mean I can't be worried too." Ashton wrung the cloth out again, laying it across her forehead. "Does this get easier?"

"Big brothering or mutants or—?" Jeevan smiled, squeezing Ash's arm as he floundered wordlessly. "You came at a crazy time. I can promise it's not always like this."

"You stitched a living bomb back together."

"Oh, I do that every fortnight." Jeevan waved it off. "Back in a tick."

He bustled off, checking on other patients on his way to the supply cupboard.

"You Yachtman's kid?" The voice made Ashton jump to his feet. Leona had sneaked up on him, leaning on Michael's arm. She licked her lips, swaying on the spot. Ashton nodded, hating that that was what he was recognised for. "I owe your sister a great debt." Leona managed a smile, falling into a coughing fit. When Michael reached for her, she waved him away, clearing her throat. "We *all* do."

She glanced at Michael, then back at Ashton. "Mike said you got her here." She smiled weakly. "I guess I owe you too." She extended her hand, surprising him and smirking at his bewilderment. "Thank you."

He shook her hand, relief washing through his chest. Michael's eyes glimmered happily.

"Back to bed, Leona." He motioned with his head. "Kathy would string me up if she knew you had moved."

"And I'm sorry to hear that, but I want to see my babies." She tipped her chin up defiantly. Michael regarded her for a moment, a man who knew when to lose.

"I'll get them. But only if you're back in your bed." Leona grinned triumphantly, pinching his cheek.

"You're a good boy," she cooed.

Michael's expression deadpanned, cheeks pinkening. He determinedly did not look at Ashton, Leona cackling and cooing some more.

"Stop it." Jeevan laughed, returning to playfully smack her hand away. "To bed, off you go."

"Oh, yessir." Leona saluted, going boss-eyed and sticking her tongue out. Jeevan shooed them away.

Ashton saw he was holding a small Tupperware tub. It contained the green paste Finn had applied to Violet's face.

"That's never coming out," he thought aloud.

167

Jeevan saw where he was looking and laughed.

"I'm convinced Finn has a secret stash of these. Like Mary Poppins' bag, but all tubs. And sweets." He popped the lid off, scooping paste onto his first two fingers. "Leona's my cousin's wife," he said, smearing the green goop on Violet's cheek. "She's family."

Ashton stared at him, not sure what to say. A sheepish smile crossed the medic's features, and he shrugged a shoulder. "Mira would mount my head on her wall if anything happened to her."

"Why didn't—?"

"I help her?"

Ashton nodded.

Jeevan grimaced. "Finn and Kathy have been doing this longer than me. They've—they've worked around that poison a few times."

"I'm sorry."

"You're not to blame for Yachtman's cruelty." He shook his head. "I know Marlon's been a dumb-dumb, but he's one of those blokes that won't talk about their feelings. Too 'manly'." He rolled his eyes. "He has a lot to work out, he just has to admit that first." He clipped the lid back on. "There we go."

Violet's face was dotted with green, but most of the medicine had been rubbed in. Her frown had already eased, usual colour returning.

"She'll probably wake up around lunch. Prepare for her to be hungry. *Hungry, hungry.*" His eyes widened warningly, and he dropped his voice to a dramatic whisper. "I've heard of mutants becoming *so* hungry, they eat their *siblings*."

"Jeevan!" Michael's voice scolded. "We do *not* belittle

ourselves with human stereotypes!"

Jeevan smirked, dashing off to join Leona.

A petite woman stood beside her, crying and smiling and kissing her cheek, arms around her neck. The woman had rich brown skin, her hair wrapped in a chunni, still in her pyjamas. Leona beamed under the attention, although a little teary-eyed herself, a twin in each arm, about six months old. Too young to know better.

Michael tutted. "Honestly," he said. "I swear he tries to make up for Finn sometimes."

"I'm sorry I yelled at you," Ashton said.

"You're forgiven." Michael smiled, tucking his hands in his pockets. "I'm not one to hold grudges, Ash. Not for little things like that."

He hunched his shoulders, gaze slipping past Ashton to Violet. "From a scientific point of view, she is *fascinating*."

His eyes sparkled with excitement; Ashton could see he was trying (and failing) to contain it. "We'll train her up when she's up and about. Properly. The more she practises, the less this happens." He nodded at her.

Ash looked at her too, curling his hands in his shirt.

"Thank you. Is there—? Is there anything *I* could do? I want to help. I know I'm just a human, but—"

"Ah, I don't buy that."

"What?"

"I don't think anyone is *just* anything. Human or not, you have as much potential as anyone else here. If you find a field you would like to work in, I'll arrange it."

Ashton narrowed his eyes.

"Why *are* you so keen to help us?"

"Mm." Michael's smile faded, only a little, but still

noticeable. "There was a time when I needed the help. I didn't see an out, not for a long, long time. Oh, that's a story for another day."

He gave a laugh that wasn't quite real, waving away Ashton's unasked question. "I'm now in a position to help, properly help. I won't turn my back on those who need me." His smile returned. He hurriedly continued before Ash could speak. "Besides, you know I like a challenge." He gestured to Violet. "And you... there's something about you that's worth the trouble. I just... haven't figured out what it is yet."

He studied Ashton's face, creases forming at the corners of his eyes. Ashton could pinpoint the moment when he fell into his thoughts, biting the inside of his cheek, reluctant to interrupt. He found himself watching Michael's eyes, at first trying to decipher what he was thinking, only to get distracted by that bewitching colouration without even noticing.

"Get a room!" Leona's cackling laughter broke the reverie. Heat burned in Ashton's face, the earlier rosiness returning to Michael's. Mira swatted her wife's shoulder, shushing her.

"Let them be!" she reprimanded. "Ignore her, Mike."

"Ignore who?"

"Hey, that's just rude!"

"Can you hear something, Ash?" Michael raised an eyebrow at him, paired with a sly smile.

"No," Ashton laughed, "not a thing."

"My, my, would you look at that? Flying babies."

"Oh—" Leona blew a raspberry, drawing the noise out as long as her breath would allow, "—to you!"

Chapter Fifteen

So…

It was alive then.

David smiled to himself. *Good.*

It would make this next part *so* much more rewarding.

He had, when the alarms blared more insistently, gone to the control room, his trio of supposed soldiers pestering their colleagues on the computers for answers. They all fell quiet when David arrived, parting for him.

He looked up at the monitors, noticing the shaky index finger of the technician to his left.

On the indicated screen, a man. A *mutant*, rather, *posing* as a man. It was tall, large and solid like a mountain. It had found one of the cameras, proceeding to set fire to everything in its view, stomping the burning husks into ashen debris. The flames danced light across its skin but revealed nothing of its features. They could hear it laughing over the mic, calling him out—*Come on, Yachtman! You ain't that scary!*

"You dragged me here for this?" He grabbed the nearest technician by the throat, squeezing. "It's *one* freak," he snarled, the technician's desperate fingernails clawing red marks on the back of his hand. "*You* can't handle *one* bloody *freak?*"

He could already see, in his mind's eye, the man's lips turning blue, bloodshot eyes bulging as his lungs rattled out their last cries for air. The man was useless, tears sliding down his cheeks. David dug his fingers in, drawing him closer. "You are *worthless*," he spat. The man's lips moved. *Please...*

David did not spare him voluntarily.

The purple light spared him.

It blasted through the room, expanding outward like a ripple in a pond. They saw it for only a second, but enough to divert David's priorities. His grip weakened as his thoughts rocketed in another direction.

Two soldiers wrestled the technician away, gasping and choking and crying. David paid them no heed, closing his eyes to see the purple light cross through his memories.

This told him it *was* alive.

This told him it was *time*.

"David..."

The sob of a voice pulled him to the present.

He turned away from the array of smashed monitors, fingers twitching at the recollection of the hammer that caused the damage.

"David... please..."

With its regular occupant AWOL, David had to find someone else for the chair. He left the basement door open, for the first time since its construction.

Ten minutes later, in walked Ella, sighing after another long shift, two hours shy of sunrise. She noticed the light climbing up from the basement, a little 'oh?' of curiosity. David listened to her footsteps draw nearer, watched the door widen, Ella's silhouette inspecting the stone steps.

"Hello?" she called. "Honey, you down here?"

He was. And he was ready. Just out of sight at the bottom of the steps, he aimed the gun. Nothing lethal, a simple tranquilliser. He fired, heard her gasp as the sharp point sank into her thigh. He counted silently to ten, then he was up the stairs two at a time, catching her as she fell forward, her head thumping on his shoulder.

She awoke in the chair. The chair was sated, holding onto its new tenant with glee. He had strapped her in rather than using the normal voltage.

She was crying, eyes red and puffy, tears splashing onto her lap. Still in her uniform. Her lips moved, framing the sounds of his name, of pleas for mercy and wordless desperate wails.

The door was shut – he checked it again with a glance up the stairs – no one would hear her.

Ella coughed, seeing the shell of the man she had married. "Please, David! Please!" Her hands jerked under their restraints, knees bouncing, bound at the ankles.

He would not listen to her, made clear by the void expanding behind his eyes, the wide, blank grin. She recoiled in the seat, straining to twist her hands free.

Her heart thundered in her ears, reducing her pleas to a blubbering mess. She could only shake her head. He still came closer. He held a syringe, filled with blood. She screamed, lurching forward in the seat, one last frantic attempt to deter him.

"Are you watching?" David asked. Ella froze at his words, a sob catching in her throat. "Are you watching, freak? I know you can hear me."

Ella flinched as the needle sank into her arm. A chuckle rumbled in his chest. Steel glinted in the eyes that once held love for her.

"Are you watching?" he repeated, mouth twitching, unable to smile wider, thumb pressing on the plunger. "This is your fault."

***

Violet awoke at lunchtime, as Jeevan had predicted. What he had failed to mention was the screaming fit that scared both Ashton and Finn out of their chairs and the light bulbs of the medbay exploding, raining glass shards everywhere.

"Fire, fire!" Kathy cried, rising from the floor in a stumbling mess of pinwheeling limbs. She had a fire extinguisher by the time Ashton was up.

Finn stayed on the floor, determinedly keeping his eyes shut and yelling for Michael.

"No, not a fire!" Ashton yelped, lunging for the fire extinguisher, Kathy whisking it away faster than he could blink.

Jeevan appeared, tackling his colleague. Kathy screeched an ungodly noise, blasting Jeevan with the foamy contents.

"MICHAEL!" Finn bellowed. Violet's screaming broke off into panicked sobbing, thrashing in the bedding, unable to free herself in her terror.

Ashton scrambled to her side, yanking the blanket away, calling for her. She tensed at the sound of her name, silent as tears rolled off her chin.

"Anyone hurt?" Michael called.

"I am!"

"Anyone other than Finn hurt?"

"I am now wounded both physically *and* emotionally," Finn complained, layering his voice with upset. Jeevan spat out foam, holding Kathy in a headlock.

"Shut up, Finn."

"Shan't."

174

Michael waved his hand, golf-ball-sized orbs of light swarming the room, twenty or so of them, hovering under their broken electrical counterparts. He scanned the room, getting a series of thumbs up—he could see nothing life-threatening, just a few scratches.

Kathy tapped out, inhaling quietly when Jeevan let her go.

"Mate!" she protested. "I'll flaming – *cough, cough* – brain you!"

Jeevan, with a perfect deadpan of an expression, wiped foam from his face and flicked it at her. Michael stepped over them with instructions to clear the glass, foam and Finn off the floor.

"Violet," he said, offering her a tissue, "what's the matter?"

She stared at the tissue, brow furrowing. Her fingers shook under her chin, catching tears on her knuckles. Michael put the question to her brother with a look.

"I—I don't know."

"Vi—?"

"He's got Mum." Sharp, prickling ice filled Ash's veins. Bile rose in his throat, stomach bunching. "He's got Mum in the basement."

Michael's gaze flicked to Ashton as he wobbled. He pointed at the chair, and it scooted forward to catch its previous occupant as he fell.

Violet waited for a moment, taking in her brother's green-grey complexion and the matching colours around him. She wiped her face on her T-shirt, though a futile motion.

"What did you see?" Michael asked, solemn, barely audible.

Her face crumpled.

"He… he had… she was… chair…" Faltering, she shoved her hands over her ears with a sob. Michael bit his lip, rubbing at his forearm.

"I can see," he said, tone offering a suggestion.

Both siblings looked at him, eyes so identical, brimming with pain. Michael raised his hand, fingertips less than an inch from her forehead. "You don't have to tell me. I can see it."

"How?" Ash croaked.

Michael wavered, shifting anxiously. Ash tried not to be irritated. "Right," he sighed, "you'll explain later."

He got a nod for that, the leader not quite looking at him. "Vi?"

"Do it."

"I'll only look for the nightmare."

"It was real," Violet insisted.

Michael nodded and she bowed her head, meeting his fingers halfway. Michael took a breath, biting the inside of his cheek.

Ash watched, stunned and speechless as the pink flecks brightened, filling their irises and covering the more natural colour. Neither of them moved; Michael's eyes creasing at the corners, squinting against an unseen illumination and Violet appeared ready to drop back into sleep, not daring to blink.

Michael drew his hand away a minute later, steadying himself on the bed. The pink withdrew, settling back into its previous amalgamation. Kathy hurried over, foam-free, placing one hand on his elbow, her arm around his shoulders.

"I'm fine. Thank you," he smiled feebly.

Kathy pursed her lips, another medic supplying a chair. She steered Michael into it. "Thank you," he said again, shoulders hunching under her withering stare.

He withstood such a glower for five, six, seven seconds, looking over his glasses up at her.

"Mmph." She scrunched her nose, spinning on her heel and bustling off.

Michael waited until he was sure she was busy with something else – moving Finn to his room at the back – before placing his attention back on the siblings.

"Are you OK?" Violet asked.

"I am." The weak smile returned, now a little sickly.

"What happened?" Ashton pressed.

Michael sighed, scratching his cheek.

He recounted the nightmare, the very real nightmare, keeping his voice low.

With each word, the ice in Ash's system only grew colder. He shivered, hugging himself. He closed his eyes at the mention of the syringe. He didn't want to hear any more, but Michael was not yet finished.

"I fear that was mutant blood. He was going to inject her with it."

"It's mine," Violet interrupted. She looked at neither of them, staring at something in her palm.

"Are you sure?" Michael questioned carefully.

She nodded, hand closing into a fist.

"What... what will happen to her?"

Ashton took the tissue when Michael offered it, drying his eyes a little too harshly.

"Well, um... now, don't take this the wrong way, but if she's lucky... she'll die."

"*What*—?"

"Let me finish. If she's unlucky, she'll... she'll turn into one of us. Manmade. Agony, tenfold that of the serum."

177

"Bad medicine," Violet corrected, mumbling.

Michael nodded absently, rubbing his eyes. He could feel the weight of Ashton's incredulous, outraged stare.

"Is there anything we can do?" Ashton demanded, voice shaking with fury.

Michael said nothing. He didn't have to reply, it was written all over his face.

Ash couldn't bear to look at him, he dropped his head into his hands.

"I'm so sorry," Michael mumbled. "I'll... I'll be in my office if you need me."

He ported away. Violet started at the movement, blinking at the space he had been.

Ashton heard her shifting on the bed, only raising his head when her feet landed on the floor. She noticed him looking, tucking her hands behind her back.

"I'm sorry."

"No."

"He said—"

"It's not. He's lying. He just wants to get in your head."

"But—"

He shook his head, shutting down her counterpoint.

Fresh tears fell and he held his hands out, wrapping her in a hug the moment she leant forward.

Chapter Sixteen

Dinner came with cake and balloons, a celebration for the captured mutants' return and their good health.

There was a band in the centre of the hall, taking requests. Ashton saw the usual guitar, drums, bass and keyboard, but there was also someone with upturned saucepans and wooden spoons, someone else with a harmonica and *someone else* with a pair of jeans. He decided not to ask.

Party hats were handed out at the door, the kind with the elastic that pinched the skin and never sat straight. Violet took a green one, given a balloon to match, staring at it in fascination. Ash was given a pink hat and an orange balloon, both wrestled onto his head and into his hand.

It seemed Michael hadn't told anyone about their mum.

"Hey!" Kurtis raced over, blue hat askew.

He scooped Violet up in a hug, blowing a raspberry on her cheek. She complained wordlessly, scrubbing her face when he set her down.

She tugged on the string of her balloon, bouncing it off Kurtis' shoulder. He laughed and then turned to Ashton, crushing his spine in a hug.

Paul caught up, holding two balloons. He patted Violet's head in greeting, eating a chicken wrap.

Kurtis drew back, finally registering Ashton's expression. With kind hands, he removed Ash's hat, passing it to his friend without looking around.

"Vi, you want to fill this with marshmallows?" Paul jostled the pink hat from its string, shoving it in her face.

"We can do that?"

"Hell yeah, we can!" Paul shoved the last of the wrap in his mouth, taking her hand and leading her away.

Ashton started after them, Kurtis' hand clasping his elbow.

"She needs the distraction. You look like you need cake and a chat."

He steered Ashton to the buffet, getting them both big slices of triple chocolate cake, then over to a table, never letting go of his arm. "What's happened then?" he asked, plonking in the seat opposite his new charge.

Ash stabbed at the cake with his fork, picturing David's face. "Whoa, whoa, whoa," Kurtis caught his wrist on the ninth stab, "cutlery scratching on plate—*ow*. My ears are sensitive, please don't do that."

Ashton huffed, dropping the utensil. Kurtis examined him, a slight turn of his head in silent question, eventually removing his grip. "Is... is Vi OK?"

"Saw our 'dad' inject our mum with Vi's blood, but otherwise just peachy," Ashton grimaced a smile, fingers pinching the cake into squashed chocolatey blobs.

Kurtis blinked once, twice, mouth gaping.

Ash began eating with his fingers, grumbling as he described the nightmare, licking icing from his thumb. "She woke up screaming, the lights exploded, and Michael poked around in her head."

"Oh, did he?"

"Yep."

"Eyes go all pink?" Kurtis circled a finger at his irises.

Ashton nodded, squashing cake into a ball before eating it. "And you say our food habits are weird." Kurtis remarked with a half-hearted laugh.

Ash motioned to him, noticing Paul and Violet making their way over.

She held the pink hat upside down with both hands, a small mountain of mini marshmallows growing over the brim. "Well now," Kurtis laughed, "I sure hope you left some for everyone else. Ah, thank you," he smiled, taking a handful of sweets, her having tipped the hat towards him in quiet offer.

She sat next to her brother, tipping a pile of pink and white cubes onto his plate, swiping a glob of cake away with her forefinger.

Paul sat next to Kurtis, nudging him in greeting.

"Tina's 'bout ready to batter Barry to death with a spatula."

"Why?"

"The dumb-dumb ported into her sink. It's *everywhere*."

Violet only ate the pink marshmallows, picking each one out with care.

Three tables over, a group of friends were sucking the helium from the balloons and singing in their new pitches. Children were playing a mad game, whacking a red balloon about, chasing after it, headbutting and kicking and punching it, shrieking when it got too close to the floor.

Finn had fallen asleep in the buffet lane, leaning on the person in front. Kathy, across the room, was asleep next to Garry with two Rs, using his upper arm as a pillow. Violet lingered on them for a moment, a red line spinning between the pair.

A loud farting noise turned her head—a balloon had been

untethered, rocketing around with the rude noise, stirring up giggles. Some of the kids raced after it to catch it.

Violet followed their progress, squishing two marshmallows between her thumb and finger.

She froze when she saw the man. She didn't drop anything this time, marshmallows secure.

No one else saw him. The farting balloon whizzed over his head and the kids ran straight past him—*get it, get it!* The man didn't look at them either. He only looked at Violet, if looking was something one could do without a face.

She could see his clothes—a knee-length coat of deep purple, buttoned to the base of his throat and belted at the waist. Black trousers tucked into black boots. She could see his hair, blacker than the night sky, tousled and erratic, like he had been pushing it back constantly in frustration. She could see the colour of his skin, a soft brown. She could *not* see his face.

He was not featureless, but a blur masked him. It reminded her of people on the news, their faces blurred for protection. His face wasn't blurred for protection. She could tell that much.

Something had gone wrong for him. He was blurred because someone, something, wanted him blurred. Wanted him forgotten.

"Vi?" Ash shook her arm. "Where'd you go?"

She hummed an *I don't know.* Shrugged a shoulder. The man was still there, still looking at her.

She selected another pink marshmallow, not looking away from him either. "Don't think about him, Vi."

Questions swirled in her head. Could Ash see the man too? "He's cruel and a liar and—and he'll pay for what he did to Mum."

Oh, he was talking about David. That made more sense.

Their mother was a kind woman, always working long shifts at the hospital. Violet could always smell sanitiser and medicine when Ella came home. Her work kept her out of the house. Gave David a free run of things. Ella, the ever-loving wife, trusted him. It would *never* have crossed her mind, him hurting their children, mutant or not. Her extent of knowledge concerning Violet's treatment stretched to her dismal room and exclusion, nothing more. While Ella was busy, while she was unaware of her husband's actions, and while she was not necessarily fulfilling her motherly role in regard to her youngest, she did not deserve a death like that. No one did.

Checking her brother over in her peripheral vision, Violet could see his rage and grief and hatred boiling the air around him.

But it was softened by worried greys and dribbles of blue, reality creeping up on him.

She nodded, once, to him, picking at her sweets again.

He rubbed her back, needing the comfort as much as she did.

The man was gone now, disappearing in an understated blink. She looked around, swinging her feet under the table. Simply surveying the room. People-watching. Nothing to concern Ash or the others. She could see not see the man, but his presence tingled under her skin.

He would come back.

She just wished she knew what for.

∗∗∗

183

Jeevan sat across the desk from Michael. Michael was slumped forward in his chair, his head having met his notes with a soft *thump* a minute ago, glasses pushed atop his head.

"You should get some sleep." The medic picked fluff from his sleeve, rolling his eyes as his friend groaned. "You know the drill, Mike. This is what happens."

"Chop my head off," Michael requested; voice muffled on paper.

Jeevan waved his hand. The light had already been switched off upon his arrival; his motion had the curtains close too. The only light came from the fire, green today, burning low over the embers. "Jeevan." Michael raised his head, plonking his chin on the table and pouting, glasses slipping a little, now sitting wonky about his hairline. "Do as you're told."

"No."

"Treachery. Insubordination. Disobedient."

"I'm not chopping your head off. Do you have *any* idea how messy it is?"

The door opened behind them, Michael grimacing as the hallway light spilled in, shielding his eyes by shoving his paperwork over his face.

"Oh, he is bad," Finn replied, clicking the door shut silently. "Michael, Michael, Miiiiccchhhaaeellll…" he called in a sing-song voice, drawing closer on light feet. Jeevan stood, letting his shattered colleague have the chair. "As you should," Finn nodded once, smug, "peasant."

"I have zero problem throwing you out the window."

"Defenestration," Michael mumbled behind the paper. Finn reached across the desk, pinching the top of the sheets and gently peeling them away.

184

Michael squinted at him, blinking hard. Finn pulled his glasses down for him, adjusting them gently. "Jeevan won't chop my head off."

"While it's definitely one way to cure a migraine, I can't nepotism if you're headless."

"Your words are broken."

"Me knows," Finn grinned. He pressed his fingers to Michael's forehead, a dull stab working through his hand. "Ah, Mike... this always happens. You need to go to bed."

"Guillotine."

"Calm down, Marie."

A knock on the door interrupted them, a timid rap only sounding three times.

"I'll get it," Jeevan said, though it was clear the other two weren't in any real fit state.

He opened the door as little as possible, not seeing anyone at first. Bright ginger hair caught his attention and he looked down.

"Violet?" he marvelled. "Where's Ashton?"

"Room." She wore her pyjamas, new with a Bulbasaur pattern on the trousers, one large image of the Pokémon on the shirt.

"Does he know you're here?"

"Is Michael OK?" She tipped her chin up, searching Jeevan's eyes.

When he didn't say anything, she studied the air around him. He wasn't sure how he felt about his 'colours' being read, but there was nothing he could do to stop it. "You're worried." She bit her thumbnail. "He was in my head. Did I do something wrong?"

"No!" Jeevan said quickly, squeezing out to crouch in

front of her. "It's nothing you did," he promised, holding her shoulders, "Mike just gets like this when he does that. He—"

She tensed, startling away as though his grip suddenly hurt. "What—?"

"Have to go," she mumbled, watching something behind him. He looked, but only saw Michael's office door. "Hope Michael feels better."

He faced forward in time to see her dash off. Something cold slithered down Jeevan's spine.

"Um, hello?" A hand on his arm.

Jeevan leapt away; fists raised.

"Ah, no!" Finn had his hands up in surrender. "That is the *last* time I'm nice to *you*," he grumbled.

Jeevan blinked, mouth dry.

Finn frowned, "You OK? You've been out here ages." Jeevan started, puzzled.

"No, I—"

"Long enough for Mike to go to sleep," Finn countered. He planted his hands on his hips, leaning forward to scrutinise his colleague. "Ah," he nodded sagely, "you've lost the plot. About time," he grinned crookedly.

Jeevan pushed him back, sighing.

"You're so annoying."

"Hey, it's dinner first. I don't come cheap, you know."

***

Ashton was still asleep when Violet got back. The day had worn heavily on him, too much to compute, too much emotion, too much of everything. He had collapsed on his new bed, snoring within the minute.

The door closed soundlessly behind her, her fingertips gracing the wooden surface. Biting her lip, she scanned the room.

The curtains were still open. She went to these first, looking out. With the light off, she could see better, the night darkening the gardens beyond. There were a few solar lights dotted in flowerbeds, planted with winter foliage and conifers. This was a wildlife garden of sorts: birdhouses, feeding tables, birdbaths, bug hotels made from old pallets bundled with sticks, logs and egg cartons, hedgehog houses tucked under bushes and a pond for the fish and frogs.

She checked each section, a nagging buzz swirling in the back of her mind. Where was he? He wanted her attention, he had been behind Jeevan, his hand on the door handle. Not to go in, but to stop *her* going in. She had run to draw him away. She didn't know who he was, and she wasn't going to risk him hurting anyone. There had been more than enough hurt already.

Her eyes adjusted, finally seeing him. Not in the garden. In the window. She yanked the curtains shut, moonlight peeking through a slither of a gap, providing enough illumination to see the shapes of things. He was standing by Ashton, looking down at her sleeping brother.

"Leave him alone."

His head snapped up; Violet was startled. Her elbow bumped the curtain. The man moved away from the bed, not a noise under his footsteps. He came around the bed, advancing on her with all the casualness of one taking a walk in the beautiful scenery outside.

She clenched her fists, terror clouding, her eyes filled with tears. She kept her ground, determinedly meeting the space his

187

eyes should be. He stood less than a foot away, head bowed to inspect her.

He had no colours. No strings. He was… blank. "Are you a ghost?" She had no other explanation; it wasn't like he was offering her any information and it was the only solution her brain provided at that moment, although she hadn't seen a ghost before either. "What do you want?" Her gaze cut past him, Ashton mumbling in his sleep. Blue and grey blotted around him, splotched with green.

Movement drew her attention back, the man raising his hand. Slowly, fingers splaying, aimed at her face. "No." She took a step back, leaning away. "Stop it."

He stilled, fingers a measly inch from her skin. Moving only her eyes, she looked him up and down. "Who are you?"

His hand lowered a fraction, fingers curling, all but one. He pressed his forefinger to her chest, right over her thumping heart.

"Vi?"

She blinked. The man was gone. Ashton was still lying down, squinting for her in the dark room. "What are you still up for?" he mumbled sleepily.

"I'm… not." The lie, while only small, was bitter on her tongue. "Bathroom."

"Oh." He relaxed a little. "OK."

She climbed into her bed, pulling the covers around her, gaze flitting about the room. The man had left; the buzzing in her skull calming to a dull whine. "Vi?" She saw Ash rubbing his hands together, as if cold, turning her head to focus on the action. "Can you—? Is Mum—?"

He didn't expect a response immediately, but he could feel the answer coming. He saw her outline move, spreading her hands, palms up, waiting for something.

"It's gone." She realised. Their mother's string, Violet had wrapped it around her wrist the moment she could, despite the fraying and the rapidly decreasing brightness.

It had been a burst of colour on her joint, no weight, temperature or texture. She had not seen when it had gone. Perhaps when she had gone to see Michael. Maybe when the man stood over a sleeping Ashton.

Securing it around her wrist was a futile gesture. It was not like Leona's string. Leona had had a chance.

"OK." Ash rolled onto his side, the greys deepening around him. "Thanks, Vi."

He wanted to be alone for a minute, his back to her. Violet clutched her bedding, a heavy ball of molten lead sinking between her lungs, scanning the room again.

The man was gone, gone for the night. She would keep an eye out for him though. He knew something – good or bad, she didn't know – but he *knew* something, and he wanted to tell her.

But did she want to hear it?

Chapter Seventeen

Michael knocked on their door that morning, an hour after sunrise, waking them both up. Finn was with him, dozing where he stood, holding a tray of two bowls of Coco Pops, a jug of milk and a bowl of jelly babies.

Ash answered the door, rubbing sleep from his eyes.

"Whazzat?" he slurred.

Michael smiled uneasily.

"Can we come in?"

Behind him, Finn snored, head drooping. Michael coughed and the medic startled awake.

"Huh? What? What's going on?" He squinted at Michael. "This is your fault. I am up *too. Early,*" he growled the last word, shoving the tray at Ash, who took it, more in surprise than anything else.

Finn squeezed his way in, yawning. "Morning, Vi. Budge over." He swatted her feet under the cover.

She drew her knees up and he flopped sideways across her bed, groaning tiresomely. "Don't be a medic, Vi. I'm dying."

"Your string's fine."

"I'm *dying,*" he stressed. "Woe is me and all that."

He waited, opening an eye when she stayed quiet. "I want pity, not logic."

She reached forward and awkwardly patted his head.

"There, there."

"Mm. Close enough." He settled back down, stealing the

duvet and rolling himself up in it.

Ash passed Violet her bowl, pouring the milk in it for her. He kept the jelly babies out of her reach, but she kept her eye on them curiously.

Michael had closed the door, standing awkwardly by it, as if prepared to bolt at any second.

"So," Ashton sat on the edge of his bed, pouring milk onto his cereal, "what have we done this time?"

"Nothing." Michael assured, a quick flash of a smile that did nothing to allay concerns. He shot a glance at Finn, who was unhelpfully asleep, and sighed. "OK, fine. I figured we – well, *I* –" he glowered at his friend, "—should tell you what Yachtman's done. I didn't want you going down to breakfast and facing it all."

Ash stirred his cereal, watching the chocolate colour the milk.

"We know about Mum."

"String's gone," Violet mumbled, wiping milk from her chin. Michael pressed his hands together.

"I'm so sorry," he said. He waited for a moment before continuing. "Yachtman has... released a story. To the media. He..." he hesitated, taking a deep breath when Ashton frowned. "I'll show you," he decided, clapping once. He caught a tablet, tapping on the screen for a moment. "Here." He walked forward, handing Ash the device.

Violet watched her brother as he read, seeing the anger form both on his face and in the reddish-brownish colour burning around him. His cereal bowl hit the carpet, tossing chocolatey milk and soggy Coco Pops everywhere.

He reached the end, launching the tablet across the room with a yell. Michael said nothing as the device shattered and fell to the floor in pieces.

Ash was now on his feet, pacing furiously, fists clenched and shaking.

Finn woke up, sitting up groggily, half-losing the duvet at the movement.

"He can't – How dare – those are *lies*—"

"Of course, they are," Michael agreed. "He knows exactly what he's doing."

"But—"

"What's he done?" Violet asked, placing her bowl on the bedside cabinet.

"You," Ash spun on his heel, smiling tightly, "are essentially a changeling child who killed his newborn daughter, escaped his mercy of treating you like his own regardless, kidnapping *me* in the process, only to later sneak back and poison Mum with your blood and…"

His voice cracked. The words would not come, but she heard them anyway.

She had killed their mother.

She looked at Michael, who inclined his head, grim, and then to Finn, still half-asleep, but gradually picking up a solemn alertness.

"He's a git, ain't he?" He stifled another yawn.

"Not the word I'm thinking of," Ash grumbled, resuming his pacing. He began chewing on his thumbnail, dots of blues and greys poking through the red-brown.

Violet followed his progress for a moment, turning the update over in her head.

Ash passed by Michael, twisting round to walk by him again. Each time, he blocked Michael from her view, only for a moment. On the fifth pass, Michael no longer stood alone, making her jump.

The man was back, standing so close behind Michael, almost on his shoulder. Michael didn't see or feel him there, he was watching Ashton fume and curse under his breath.

She could feel the weight of the man's stare from behind the blurred features.

"What?" she asked, freezing up, having forgotten about her company.

All three of them were staring at her. Michael took a few steps towards her, yellow bubbling around him. The man followed, staying close.

"What, what?" Finn asked, poking her shin.

She looked down. Their strings were on the floor. Finn didn't have a red one, but his yellow was almost as strong as Michael's, zigzagging around him. She hadn't looked at Finn's strings before, the realisation surprising her. How had she not noticed them before?

She reappraised the man. Still without colours or lines. "Hey." Finn poked her again. "Earth to Violet, come in, Violet. You there?"

"Yes."

"What, what then?" The man raised his hand, hovering by Michael's elbow. "Has Mike gone a funny colour? That why you're staring at him?"

She managed a shake of her head. The man was pointing down, bobbing his hand insistently.

Michael half-turned at the waist, searching the room behind him. His gaze travelled over the man one, two, three times. The man seemed to look at him, stilling almost expectantly.

When Michael turned back to Violet, befuddled, the man

continued pointing down.

Weight shifted the bed next to her. Ashton.

"Tell me you don't believe him." Low voice, hoarse. A wobble of grief he couldn't hold much longer.

"Who? Oh, him," she realised, answering her own question before he registered it.

The image of their mother popped into her head, pleading, hysteria breaking her voice. Violet rubbed at her forehead, a hot needle driving into her temple, inhaling a brittle, tiny breath.

The man touched his head, in the same place her pain was, still pointing at the floor with the other hand.

"What *are* you looking at?" Michael puzzled, shifting uncomfortably. He checked behind him again. Still nothing. He opened his mouth, a question scattered across his face.

The man lay his hand on Michael's shoulder, the questioning look rippling away into a serene thoughtfulness.

"Uh oh, you broke Michael," Finn muttered. His head swivelled, squinting suspiciously at the siblings in turn. "You two keep breaking Michael. I don't appreciate it."

"We should start Vi's training today," Michael announced, decision in his tone, expression lit with an empty light.

Finn and Ashton exchanged scepticism. The man took his hand away and Michael blinked, brow creasing slightly. "Yes, I think... I think today's the day. What do you think, Violet?"

The man nodded. Violet found herself nodding too. Michael smiled. "Cool. I'm going to grab some stuff. Check something. Finn, can you bring them down to Class One when they're ready? Thanks."

"You didn't even – Don't walk away when I'm talking – MICHAEL!"

The door closed. The man remained. Finn swore under his breath. "Don't repeat that, Vi."

***

Class One was empty, but at half seven in the morning, sane and un-Michaeled people were either at breakfast or – teasingly – still asleep.

Finn threw himself onto the chair behind the desk, his momentum spinning the seat. On the third rotation, he was out like a light.

Class One was much like any other classroom: seven tables, some with four chairs, some with six chairs, each one prepped with a caddy of pens and pencils and rulers and anything else the kids would need. Brightly coloured drawings and comprehensive work filled the walls, hand-painted suncatchers hanging in the windows, twirling slowly. There were holiday decorations, all handmade and childishly, roughly designed on the windowsills and the walls, some even from the ceiling.

There were bookshelves and storage units, one chocker and one awaiting the belongings of the students. The whiteboard still had yesterday's lesson on it—*Move it or Lose it, An Intro to Telekinesis.*

The door opened. Michael walked in. The man was two steps behind him. He had disappeared at some point, en route to the classroom. Violet studied him for a second—whatever he had done to Michael, he clearly wanted to see it through.

"You can sit down." Michael smiled.

Violet quickly checked him over, but the man wasn't meddling here. Michael was Michael.

Ash sat on the edge of the nearest table, folding his arms across his chest. Violet pulled out a chair and sat next to him, slightly behind him. Michael caught Finn's chair by the headrest, considering his sleeping friend for a moment. A sly smile spread across his lips. "EEAAARTTHQUUAAAKEE!" he shouted, shaking the seat erratically. Finn yelped, toppling sideways out of the chair in a windmill of limbs and disappearing under the desk with a *thump*.

"I. *Hate*. You," he part-groaned, part-growled. Michael smiled innocently, hands on his knees to inspect and snicker at his friend. "Oh, I'm fine by the way!" Finn sulked, projecting his voice to include the siblings. "No need to rush to my aid!"

"Oh, OK then." Ashton shrugged.

Michael grinned lopsidedly at him. Ash raised an eyebrow. "So... now you've terrorised Finn—"

"Always the priority."

"—why are we... here?" Ash gestured at the classroom. He hadn't quite imagined such a normal setting for Violet's training—maybe a magical dojo or an arena or something. Somewhere the mutants could blast and zap and frog each other.

Michael adjusted his glasses, leaving Finn on the floor to sit on the front of the desk. The man sat next to him, mimicking his pose – arms folded, legs crossed at the ankles – except for the position of his head: tilted, aiming his blurred face at Violet, waiting. His fingers drummed on his arm.

"Class One is where we first start teaching the kids. Powers properly start developing around the ages of seven to ten, it varies on abilities and heritage and blah blah blah." Michael rolled his hand as he spoke.

Finn finally got up, using the desk as leverage. He made

a face at the back of Michael's head, flopping sulkily into the chair, spinning again. Michael smirked before continuing. "I figured we'd get here a tad early—"

"*A tad?*" Finn protested, rotating away and muttering.

"—and show Vi around before the other kids come in with all their racket."

Michael scrunched his nose. "Vi, most of your classes will be in here. This is where you'll learn your primary abilities. Uh," he scratched his chin, "the rest will... well, I thought I'd help you there."

"Study," Finn corrected, folding his arms on the desk to go back to sleep.

"No, I mean... maybe a bit. Look, it's a win-win, we both learn something." Michael half-laughed, scratching his ear.

Finn just grunted, burying his head in his arms. "You're no help." Michael sighed. "Come on, you two. We'll carry on without Misog here."

Michael led them out. Violet held Ashton's hand, her shoulder bumping his arm on every other step. The man walked beside her, uncomfortably close. Making sure she followed whatever idea he had put in Michael's head.

Michael explained the other classes to them, pointing at each door in turn. The numbers corresponded with the floors— Class Two was elemental; Class Three was for the shapeshifters and so on. There was a large hall for sports. A second large hall for combat and weapons training. A fully stocked gym, a few early birds calling out greetings as they lifted weights and pedalled on exercise bikes. A small library down here, mostly for the kids.

Michael turned left, the uncanny school hallways snapping into rocky tunnels, sloping downwards and lit with humming electric lanterns on the walls.

"Down here is for the rockies, our biggest elemental group. Each element gets a place to play, we'll come to them in a bit."

Ash and Violet exchanged looks. OK, so water and plants, yeah sure. That was imaginable. Fire? Electricity? *Air*? Air was everywhere, how was that supposed to be a special play area? And if the rockies had tunnels, what did the burners have, *Hell*?

Michael smiled knowingly. "We manage."

The tunnel continued to slope for another ten, fifteen minutes. Violet rubbed at her ears, eyeing the rocky ceiling every few seconds. Michael patted her head reassuringly. "We're almost there."

The man picked up the pace at this, falling in step beside Michael.

"Almost where?" Ashton asked, cringing away from the walls pressing in on either side of him. "Why are we down here? What's this got to do with Vi?"

"Part of the tour," Michael replied distantly. Violet looked at him, seeing the man's hand on his elbow.

A minute later, the tunnel opened into a large, rough circle of a cavern. More tunnels stretched out on the other side. Piles of rubble and boulders were all around the cavern. Someone had built a statue of themselves, although the head had been knocked clean off and replaced with an oven-sized boulder.

"We put the rockies down here because it's quieter. For us. If you ever come down here during rockball—"

"Rockball?"

"Um… like if dodgeball and basketball had a baby and that baby was born with mountains in each hand."

"Sounds cool."

"It is, just not on the ears."

Seeing Ashton's interest, Michael began relating events of the last rockball game. Violet wanted to listen too – exactly the kind of mad game she had come to expect of this place – but the blurred-faced man had other ideas.

He waved to her, for her attention, and began to walk, aiming for the third tunnel on the left. He got about halfway, half-turning to beckon her on. Her feet moved of their own accord, but she forgot to let go of her brother.

His fingers tightened around hers, drawing her to a stop.

"Stay close," he said. "I don't want you lost in those tunnels."

The man motioned to her again, impatient. Violet dithered, looking between him and Ashton. "Is this… another line thing?" Ash asked. He was trying. Really, really trying.

But he was also struggling, evident in the blue, grey, red-brown swirling around him. He hated this cavern.

Another beckon. Violet pointed to the tunnel.

"Need to go that way," she said.

"Why?" Both Ash and Michael asked.

Violet hesitated. Ashton groaned, a drawn-out noise that signalled he was regretting his decision already. "OK, fine. We'll go. But do *not* let go of me."

"I won't." She squeezed his hand. He smiled, relieved at the confirmation, and he squeezed back.

As soon as he saw them following, the man relaxed and started to walk again. Violet led the other two after him, determinedly not taking her eyes from their guide.

About twenty feet in, they began to lose their light. Michael sighed, drawing circles in the air with his finger. Each circle produced a golf-ball-sized light orb, forming a trail marking their route.

"The rockies dig, collapse and excavate new tunnels every day. The cavern stays the same, but this?" He gestured around them. "All new. All the time." Violet could feel his quizzical look on the back of her head. "Where are we going, Vi?"

The man took a left turn, into a far narrower tunnel. They had to walk in single file, turning sideways at some points to squeeze through. Ash's hold tightened on her hand.

"I don't like this," he mumbled. "I don't like this; I don't like this."

Violet glanced back for just a second, green spiking through his other colours.

Behind him, Michael stretched out his arm, fingertips applying an ever so slight pressure on Ashton's shoulder. His eyes widened. The green faded, the red-brown softened into almost pastel hues.

The man took another left, then a right, down another slope. This opened into another cavern, half as wide as the first one, ceiling a couple of feet above Ashton's head.

"Better?" Michael asked.

"A smidge." Ash grimaced a smile, rubbing his chest. "How do you do that?"

"You changed his colours," Violet mumbled.

The man had stopped in the middle of the cavern, looking down at his feet.

"I did?" Michael tapped his chin. "I suppose so," he mused. At their questioning looks, he smiled, somewhat bashful. "Finn calls me a brainhacker. I can, um… I can snoop into people's brains. Not in…" He shook his hands, wriggling his fingers like a puppeteer. "Not mind control. Contrary to

200

popular belief, we can't actually do that."

"Brainhacking sounds like mind control," Ashton remarked.

"I can change people's emotions. Only to calm them down, temper or anxiety or the likes. I... won't use it for anything else."

He cast his gaze down, an unreadable look flitting through his eyes. "I can see memories, dreams, that sort of thing, but I... I've never used it to pry. I ask first, you know. And... I don't use it often either, I—"

"Is that why you were ill?" Violet butt in. "Jeevan said you were ill."

"Um... yes. You... came to see me?"

"Are you better now?"

"I am. The migraines only last a day or so, bit less with the meds' help."

Michael turned his attention to the cavern, eyes sweeping over the walls, up to the ceiling and then back down to Violet. "Why did you come to see me? Did you need help with something?"

"And does it have something to do with why we're here?" Ash was picking at his lip, a little peaky.

Violet nodded. They waited for her to elaborate, Ashton exasperating when she turned away.

The man was watching them again, still in the centre. Noticing Violet, he pointed down. The same motion as before, insistent and repetitive. Down, down, down.

"What's down there?" she asked, pointing at the ground beneath the man's feet.

"Erm... I believe the rockies don't dig deeper than this." Michael rubbed his jaw, eyes blazing with thoughts behind his glasses. "What do you see?"

She scratched her nose, sniffing and looking away. Ash puffed out his cheeks.

"Is avoiding questions a mutant thing?"

"Ha-ha," Michael deadpanned. "You should go into stand-up."

"I just might." Ashton tapped his sister on the head. "Use words. Leave rocks. Fresh air. Now please."

"Mm…" Michael hummed when Violet still didn't respond. He followed her gaze, looking straight at the man and still not seeing him. "OK. I'll get one of the rockies, see if they can help."

Ashton's hand shot out, latching onto his arm. He was paler, eyes widening in alarm.

"You are my quick ticket out of here," he hissed. "Do *not* leave me down here."

"I'll only be—"

"*Nope*." Ash shook his head frantically, fingers squeezing. "You're staying here. This all collapses, *you* are getting us out of here."

"OK, OK." Michael patted his hand, relieving the hold a little, but not freeing himself from it. "I can get a message to Finn, but it'll take longer." He raised an eyebrow. "You want to stay down here *longer*?"

Ashton swallowed dryly, biting his lip, another shake of his head.

"You can go," Violet encouraged gently, swinging his hand.

"I'm not leaving you down here."

"You're scared."

"Something to that effect."

"Wait upstairs."

"No." His grip constricted on them both. He was trembling, but now determination brought some colour back to his face. "I'm staying here. Just... hurry up with this, please?"

Violet looked back at the man. Still pointing down. She studied the cavern floor, unsurprisingly not seeing anything.

"Let's go," she decided. The man waved his hands in protest, stomping his foot when she took Michael's hand. "Can ask upstairs?"

"Are you sure?" Ashton asked, smoothing a loose lock of her hair back from her face.

She didn't need to look at his colours to see his relief. She nodded and he exhaled, giving a small smile. "You heard the lady, Mike. *Exeunt.*"

They ported, returning to Class One. Finn was still asleep in the chair, but he now had company. A woman, late twenties maybe, with mouse-brown hair tied back in a ponytail. She wore a blue knitted cardigan with daisies stitched in the pockets, a knee-length black skirt and white tights. Her trainers were white, well-worn, with rainbow-coloured laces.

"Oh!" she said, eyes widening in surprise at their appearance. Her hand froze mid-writing on the whiteboard. "Hello." She capped her pen, straightening her large, rounded glasses. "Morning, Michael."

"Good morning, Pepper. How are you?"

"My chair has been stolen," she clicked her tongue at Finn, "but I'm well. Yourself? I heard you weren't tiptop yesterday."

"Oh, I'm fine." He waved it off. He gestured to the siblings. "This is Ashton and Violet." Pepper smiled, waggling her fingers in greeting.

"Nice to meet you both. Are you joining us today, Violet?"

Violet looked at the board behind her – *Be there or be square, porting for B* – That was as far as she had got. Pepper tapped the pen on her hand, smiling kindly. Her colours were soft yellows and oranges, like the latter end of a sunset.

Her strings—the blue one was strong with a steady glow. Her red stretched out beyond the room. Her yellow was vibrant too, though not as much as Michael's, but still rather sustainable. It rolled in patterns above her head, like a thought bubble.

"Vi?" Ash poked her head, leaning down to catch her eye. He looked content up here, but she could see he was itching to sprint out the door and enjoy wide open spaces and fresh air. "You want to stay for a bit? Check it out?" He offered an encouraging smile. "Could be fun."

"We'll be porting to the kitchens." Pepper dropped her voice to a secretive whisper. "They're making cupcakes today, so we'll be stealing them."

"Um—" Michael held up a finger.

"You heard nothing." Pepper insisted. "Now, take this," she jabbed her pen at Finn, "and shoo. It's our cake day, not yours."

"Save me a chocolate one and I'll say nothing."

"You are easily swayed," she joked, eyes sparkling. "Deal."

Chapter Eighteen

Michael accompanied Ashton on his walk out into freedom. They ventured into the wildlife gardens that Ash could see from room five-sixteen. The air was clean. He could smell winter flowers. Birds were singing. The wind was icy but refreshing. He slung off his coat, enjoying the chill on his bare skin. He filled his lungs, spreading his arms, coat folded over his right forearm.

"I will never go back inside."

"Food is inside."

"I may sometimes go back inside," he rectified. "Will Vi be all right?"

"Pepper's our best teacher. She'll have Vi porting about in no time."

"Regardless of the fact that they're stealing cupcakes?"

"I prefer to think of it as *liberating*," Michael nodded. When Ashton didn't look impressed, he sighed. "Look, they're really nice cupcakes."

"I don't care. It's – still – stealing." With each word, he jabbed Michael in the chest.

"Sooooo... stealing is bad?" Michael guessed.

"Yes." Ashton poked him again.

"Welp, there go my weekend plans to rob the government." He sighed dejectedly, shoulders slumping.

Ash tutted, flourishing his coat out behind him. It was much like what Kurtis and Paul wore that day they had found him and Violet. He tucked the hood over his head and let it hang from there.

"You are a corrupt leader. Nepotism and taking bribes and… unpatriotic-like behaviour."

"Don't get me started on the government." Michael shook his head. "I don't have the energy for that today."

Ash decided not to argue with that, and they began walking again. Michael zipped his coat up the last little bit, beneath his chin. He shoved his hands in his pockets. "Are you all right?"

"Better up here." Ash rubbed some warmth back into his face, the cold sweeping it away in a heartbeat. He sensed the weight of Michael's gaze on him, could almost hear the cogs whirring, spewing out thoughts. "I'm angry," he admitted, concentrating ahead of them. "I… don't believe it."

"That he would do that? Or that it happened?"

"Yes." A bird shot from a treetop, circling away, chirping. Ash watched it flap away, sighing. "And then… to blame *Vi?* He's—he's nothing but a *coward*."

"People like him often are." Michael was watching the bird too. "I lost my mum when I was a kid. I don't remember her, not really."

"I'm sorry."

"Mm. Can't grieve what I didn't know."

"You can." Ashton nodded. "You really can." Michael bit his lip, quiet for a moment.

"What was she like? Your mum?"

"Kind. Bit scatty, but I guess that comes from having six kids." Michael gave a little 'hmmph' of agreement.

Ashton wiped his hands on his shirt, hesitating.

"What is it?"

"What…? What do you… what do you think he's done with her—*her*?"

"Mm." Michael tucked his nose into his coat. "Hard to tell," he admitted, voice muffled. "Forgive me for speaking so bluntly, but he has already used her death to attack Violet. He may use her funeral for a similar motive."

Ashton stopped in his tracks. Michael got three steps ahead before realising. "Ash?"

"I never said goodbye to her. I'll *never* say goodbye to her."

He didn't realise he was crying until Michael handed him a tissue. He could not voice his thanks, nodding numbly instead. His companion gently steered him, hand warm on his arm, to sit on the grass. The ground was softer on the greenery, but still rather cold.

Ashton dabbed at his eyes, wiped his nose. Michael conjured up a box of tissues, extra-large. "I'm—I'm sorry." Ash hiccupped.

"For what?" Michael straightened the top tissue. Ash gestured at himself, blowing his nose. Michael smiled grimly. "Don't apologise for sincerity. It's hard to find these days."

He stretched out his hand, hesitating for a moment, before patting Ash's knee. His hand remained there, keeping his eyes on Ashton's face. "If you weren't angry… if you weren't upset or – or grieving, if you pushed this all down – you'd be hurting yourself more. Let your brain do its thing."

"My brain hates doing its thing."

"Hey, mine too." Michael half-laughed. Ash took another tissue.

"Thought that *was* your thing."

"Shh, you'll blow my cover." He put a finger to his lips,

eyes sparkling with mischief.

Ashton sniffed, managing a watery smile. Michael's hand moved to his shoulder, squeezing. "Cry if you need to. It's only the fish that'll judge you and they're over there." He waved vaguely, the pond a fair distance away.

"Make jokes when you're nervous?"

"I wouldn't call them *jokes* exactly… but I try."

Michael summoned tea for them. A large flask of it, delightfully warm, accompanied by packets of sugar and little pots of milk, two mugs, two teaspoons and a plate of assorted biscuits. He poured two sugars and a milk pot in one, stirring and then passing it to Ashton. "Fun fact about me—my brainhacking lets me know how people like their tea."

"You are every British person's dream."

"Pretty sure the Chinese have had tea a lot longer than us, but thanks." Michael grabbed up several sugar sachets – seven? Eight? – tearing them open all at once and dumping their contents in his mug. He stirred, tapped his spoon twice on the side, and silence settled over them.

They sat and watched the gardens around them, listened to a winter breeze rustle the trees and the shrubs, a bird trilling somewhere in the distance.

Michael dipped a digestive in his tea, sighing through his nose when it broke and sank into the brown depths. "Drown then," he mumbled. Ash gave a soft laugh, reaching for a custard cream. Michael salvaged only some of his biscuit, electing to replace it instead. His hand bumped Ashton's. "Oops," he said, darting away the same time Ashton did. "You first."

"No, it's OK. You go."

"No, you."

"You."

"I insist."

"I desist."

"They're all mine then." Michael swiped the remaining digestives, a chocolate bourbon and a custard cream. The same custard cream Ashton had gone for, resulting in them both clinging to a single biscuit. "Um, excuse me." Michael raised an eyebrow. "You desisted."

"Irrelevant. You put custard creams in front of me, I *will* eat them all." The captive biscuit snapped in half, crumbs showering down between them. "Huh. I guess that works too." He wolfed his half down before Michael snatched that as well.

Michael pouted at his portion. "Let me help you with that," Ashton said. Quick as a flash, he 'liberated' the remnant, Michael gaping at him in betrayal as he chewed it victoriously.

"After all I've done for you…" He sniffed haughtily. Ashton nudged him. Michael turned his nose up with a 'hmmph!'

He 'sulked' while they finished their teas – his didn't take long, being ninety-percent soggy crumbs – but Ash could tell he wasn't mad, not really. He set his mug down.

"Thanks, Mike."

"That biscuit's going to cost you. Fiver."

"I'll buy my own. Thanks," Ashton smiled weakly. Michael thumbed his nose at him, corners of his mouth twitching. Ash began to speak. Michael beat him to it.

"I want to show you something."

"Oh, Seltik…"

"Have a little faith, mate." Michael held his hand out, palm up. Ash narrowed his eyes at it.

"Bring the biscuits and it's a deal."

Michael sighed, retrieving the plate with his free hand.

He wriggled his outstretched fingers. Ashton saw the biscuits were secured and obliged, squeezing his eyes shut.

His stomach twisted as Michael ported. He opened his eyes to a minor queasy feeling.

"See?" Michael smiled. "You're getting used to it."

"Bleh." Ashton poked his tongue out.

Michael replied in kind. "Where are we?" Ashton asked, helping himself to another biscuit.

They stood in a large cylindrical room. Hundreds and thousands of candles of all shapes, sizes, scents and styles burned in front of tiny windows—no, not windows. Framed photographs, hung on the wall or stood on shelves, shimmering in the candlelight.

The floor was decorated with mosaics, the colours and pictures changing—all kinds of animals and scenery and people and patterns. A lily unfolded under his feet, tiles fluttering into a horse galloping away, across an unfurling green field. In the centre of the room, a brazier, burning with a fire taller than him and as varied in colour as the floor beneath them.

Michael shed his coat, folding it neatly into a bundle and placing it tentatively on the floor, next to the plate he had already set down. Ash did the same, lifting the hood from his head. "What is all this?" he asked.

"It's our Memory Hall."

"Where's the ceiling?"

"Somewhere up there." Michael craned his head back. Despite the candles rising higher than it felt possible, the light or their vision simply did not travel far enough. "This has been here as long as we have. It expands when we need it to, but it changes nothing outside."

"Like the Tardis?"

"We had a vote—we are not allowed to call it the Tardis." He shrugged a shoulder. "But yes, a similar thing." He let go of Ashton's hand, taking a few steps to the left. He pointed at a photo on the wall. "That's my uncle," he said, looking over his shoulder. Ash took that as an invitation to follow.

"Is that you?"

"Yes, that's me," Michael sighed. His fingertips traced his uncle's grinning face. The photograph was old, Michael no more than six, missing a front tooth from his bright smile. He sat on his uncle's shoulders, clasping a book to his chest. His uncle was a tall, broad, white man, with messy black hair and hazel eyes creased at the corners. He wore a pale blue shirt, top button undone, sleeves rolled up, pens in the pocket. "We were going to a book signing," Michael said. "I was so excited; I hardly slept the night before. I wanted to meet the author so badly."

"Who—?"

"They wrote a book offering several different theories on mutant existence and their compatibility with the human world."

"You read that when you were…" Ashton circled a finger at the picture, "how old?"

"I turned six about four months after this was taken." He tapped the picture, a fond smile lighting his eyes. Behind them, the fire crackled, casting a pink glow across the tiled floor. Books and pens made their way across the mosaic, the books flipping their pages, the pens leaving words in an inky trail in their wake. Ashton stared at the letters, but it wasn't a language he recognised.

"We remember all sorts in here, Ash. Good memories, bad memories, ambitions and ideas, the living and the lost."

Ashton let his attention wander over some other frames. Pictures of families, he recognised a few faces.

He saw diplomas and birth certificates, in-memorias and congratulations. Cards from dozens of different celebrations, graduation photos and baby scans.

He found another one of Michael, about halfway around the room. Eight maybe, on a crazy golf course with the sea glittering in the background, a cheery sunny day. Little Michael had a look of utmost concentration, lining up his shot. Behind him crouched a young Finn, arms and legs covered in plasters decorated with dinosaurs. He too was concentrating— concentrating on sneaking his club between Michael's feet to hook it on his friend's club and throw off his shot.

Movement next to him, Michael stifling a bemused sigh. "He was always a terrible cheat. He's even worse now."

"That doesn't sound like Finn," Ash denied, tone full of mock disbelief. Michael scoffed.

"Uncle Bobby found Finn. He was... don't repeat what I'm going to tell you, to anyone. *Especially* Finn. OK?"

Ashton nodded, crossing his heart for extra measure. Michael pressed his lips together, contemplating him for a second.

Then, eventually, he nodded. "OK," he said. "My uncle found Finn, the sole survivor of one of Yachtman's raids. Finn doesn't... doesn't really remember. Uncle Bobby said his brain tried to forget, but sometimes..." Michael shook his head. "Finn was found under his mother's body. He was only six. Uncle Bobby brought him back. He looked after Finn himself. It took seven months for him to get a word out of him.

You know what he said?"

"What?"

"Sorry."

"Sorry? Why—? Why was he—?"

"Like I said, his memories of the raid are fuzzy at best. He didn't get why Uncle Bobby was looking after him. He just knew he had been taken away from his home. Thought he'd done something wrong. So..." Michael rocked on the soles of his feet, hands in his pockets, "he apologised."

He looked at the photo again. "I knew about Finn long before I met him. Uncle Bobby had him for about a year, year and a half, before we met. This golf day, this was our first day trip out. That was the day we really became friends."

"Even though he was cheating?"

"I... wasn't very good at making friends when I was little. My uncle said it was the cons of being clever. Finn was the first person I'd met that was on par with me. He was a challenge. *Is* a challenge," he corrected with a laugh, "such a *nuisance*."

"See, now that *really* does sound like Finn."

"We needed each other. I was lonely. He was alone. He became the brother I never had." Michael smiled, a little sad, but also content. "I wouldn't change him for the world. Well..." Michael thought for a moment. "Maybe shrink his ego a little, but hey." He shrugged. "The only way of doing that is decapitation. I've heard that's messy stuff though." His gaze drifted past Ashton, eyes widening. "Look!" He pointed back towards the photo of himself and his uncle— the frames on the wall were shifting, sliding up or down or to the side, revealing an empty spot.

Michael was smiling, a hand on Ash's arm and guiding him back. "The hall's giving you a space."

"For—? What? I—I can put—?" He aimed a shaky finger at the wall. Michael nodded. "I... I don't have a picture of her."

"No need. This is the *Memory* Hall. Think of her and the Hall will produce it."

Ash closed his eyes. He thought of the last time he had seen his mother, at the dinner table, checking his head for injuries after his supposed mugging. The air tingled with a gentle warmth before him, washing over his skin as he sifted through his memories.

He opened his eyes when Michael squeezed his arm.

When he was little, his nana had a caravan, Norfolk way. He was four in the picture, Rose not yet two. He stood on the cushioned bench that framed two sides of the dining table. She was in a highchair, upending a bowl of baked beans over herself and the tray. Their mother stood over them, reaching for the baby with one hand, laughing and wincing at the mess. With the other hand, she held Ashton by the back of his *Thomas the Tank Engine* shirt.

"That's the first holiday I remember," he told Michael, voice no louder than a mumble. "I, um... Nana got this picture. Mum let me go to get Rose and I... I fell. Right into all that." He wriggled a finger at the baked bean mess. "It went *everywhere*. We were late to meet our aunt because we both needed a bloody good bath." He folded his arms, holding onto his elbows. "I liked that day. Nana's caravan only had a shower. Mum stood us both in the cubicle, said she was the Mess Police. Made *pew-pew* noises with the shower."

He concentrated on Ella's face. A tired mother of two under-fives, but happy with their little life, amused and exasperated at their adorable mishaps. Ash felt his smile fade. "He didn't come with us on that holiday. We got home and he was so happy."

Michael thought for a second.

"That would be about the time the AMCD came to be. Wouldn't it?"

Ashton nodded glumly. Michael looked at Ella again. "She's beautiful."

"She is."

The candlelight flickered around them, momentarily darkening their vision. When it normalised, an unlit candle stood on the shelf below the new photograph. Michael summoned a matchbox, offering it to Ashton.

It took him four tries to strike a match, hands shaking so, but he lit the candle unaided. "Goodbye, Mum."

Chapter Nineteen

Finn was sitting on Michael's desk when they entered. He was reading, although the book looked like it was upside down.

"There are chairs *right there*," Michael sighed.

Finn hummed in agreement, turning the page. "Why are you—?" Michael bowed as he walked forward, squinting at the title. Ashton followed normally, upright, plonking down in one of the chairs. He couldn't read the title on the spine, but it looked similar to the language on the mosaics in the Memory Hall.

Finn passed the book to Michael as he flopped down in his chair, revealing a lolly stick poking from his mouth. He examined Ash's face for a moment, removing the sweet and pointing at him with it.

"Your sister," he scolded, "ported right onto my *head*." Ashton coughed a laugh, hurriedly clearing his throat when Finn glowered. "We crashed into a medicine cupboard and Kathy's making me do stocktake *again*."

"Is Vi OK?"

"I took her back to class. I'm great, though, thanks for asking."

"Ooh." Michael leant forward in his chair. He nudged Finn in the back until the medic scooted off the table and into the seat beside Ashton. "I was looking for this," Michael said, lying the book on the desk. "Where'd you find it?"

"It was stopping our desk from wobbling."

"It was—" Michael blinked. Finn stared at him evenly, tapping a beat with his forefinger on the arm of his chair. "You used *my* book for *what*?" Michael's voice was quiet and the look he settled on Finn promised a swift end.

"It was Jeevan's idea." Finn threw his lolly into the bin, a clean shot. Michael's mouth was a tight line.

"Oh, I don't think so. I'm not talking to you anymore."

"Shame." Finn stretched his arms over his head, stifling a yawn. "Ash, wake me up when his paddy's over." He snuggled down in the chair. Two seconds later, he was asleep, chin tucked to his chest, snoring softly.

Ashton marvelled at him.

"I wish I could fall asleep like that."

"Book damage is taken seriously here, Ash. *Very* seriously," Michael nodded, eyes wide with warning.

"I'll... bear that in mind."

"Thank you. Ooh, he's dented the cover. I'm going to *kill him*."

"Five minutes ago, you said he was the brother you never had," Ashton said.

"Cain and Abel."

"Fair. What's the book then?"

"Bruised. Oh, you meant—this is a book of... mm, not prophecies exactly. Our soothsayers have..." Michael hummed a quick tune, pushing his brain into gear. "Let's just go with predictive titbits."

Ash made sure he was comfortable in his chair before rolling his hand for Michael to continue. "OK, so, for years, soothsayers have compiled their predictions in books. I'm talking hundreds and thousands of years and thousands and *thousands* of predictions."

Ashton cast a sceptical look at the book. Probably no wider than *Watership Down,* but it did beg the question how broken that desk was.

Michael drummed his fingers on the pages. "All right, not *every* prediction is in here. Let me start again," he insisted, rubbing at his forehead. "Predictions can vary in importance. Uh, weather, your next meal, what you'll get for your birthday. Or it could be changes in the world. Here, look. A soothsayer predicted climate change in 1692." He turned the book to Ashton, who nodded dutifully though he still couldn't read it.

"Did they tell anyone?"

"Yep. Except she was burned at the stake for it, which probably didn't help the ozone layer. Anyway," he flailed a hand, getting off track, "all the most important predictions go into books like this. There are eight that I know of. I have two. This one and another that I've hidden."

"Where are the others?"

"Probably holding up Finn's tables," Michael grumbled, shooting his sleeping friend a disgusted look of betrayal. "I don't know. Two are rumoured to be destroyed, another lost to the humans. No idea on the others."

Michael began flipping the yellowed pages, humming to himself. "If I've worked it out right, this is book number five in the series. I believe one pops up every two to three centuries. Don't look at me like that—there are a *lot* of weather predictions to sift through."

He continued looking through the pages for a minute or so, scanning the lettering, searching for something. He almost reached the end when he brightened, having located whatever it was. Ash didn't notice for a few seconds, puzzled—Michael had been reading the language upside down.

Michael tapped a line of handwritten script, grinning. Ash looked down, biting his lower lip.

"Yes," Ash nodded sagely, "I see."

"You can't read it, can you?"

"No. Not at all."

"You could've just *said.*" Michael rolled his eyes. Ash shrugged apologetically. "Face." Michael demanded, holding his hands out, fingers grabbing at the air when Ashton didn't move. "Bring your face here. It's a temporary spell to read everything in your language."

"You could've just *said.*"

"Oh, ha, ha."

Ashton smirked, leaning forward. Michael pressed his hands on either side of Ashton's face, fingers bracing on his temples. He mumbled something in another language Ash didn't recognise either. A light buzzing bristled inside his head, fading away when Michael sat back.

"Oh, hello," he smiled, pulling the book closer to him, staring at the text. Everything was in English now, his gaze flitting all over the page.

He had expected poetry, like prophecies in books he had read. Instead, it was like reading someone's exam notes:

Illness of the pigs 2000s-ish?
Viral plants
Avoid 2020

Ashton pointed. "What'll happen in 2020?" Michael shrugged.

"I'm not a soothsayer. But we've got, like, thirteen years until then? It can be future Michael and Ashton's problems."

"Can't argue with that."

Ash looked at what Michael had indicated before he had placed the spell. "'A purple will rise. Could go either way. Plan for peace. Or plan for doomsday.' What?"

"When I told you purple was bad for mutants—that was a… half-lie, let's say." He swayed in his chair.

Ash read the lines again. Michael leaned forward in his seat, steepling his fingers. "Purple is a clue for something of great significance in our world." He said. "I believe the last clue we had prefaced the French Revolution."

"Really?"

"Yep. Although, I think the mutant in question didn't *glow* purple." He arched an eyebrow at Ashton. "Violet is different," he admitted, "very different. When I brainhacked her, I got— mmm, you don't just get what you went in for. The brain's too busy to be so concise. I pick up afterthoughts. Subconscious thoughts. Aspects of the person."

"Right," Ashton said uncertainly. "What did you, um, pick up from her then?"

"I'm not sure." He stopped swaying in the chair, narrowing his eyes at Finn. He jolted in his seat and Finn awoke with a yelp.

"Um…" The medic squinted, blurry-eyed. "*Ow.*"

"Now imagine how my book felt." Michael smirked. "I need your opinion on this, being the present medical expert." Finn grumbled something unsavoury, but he shifted about until both elbows were resting on the desk.

Michael nodded once, then looked back to Ash. "I picked up a few things from Violet, but it was… unclear. Like a bad radio connection. Everything was patchy."

"Told you she had a funny head."

"Now, hold on," Ashton cut in, "maybe... maybe it's 'cos he hurt her all those times or... or she's, uh, she's only just developing her powers, so maybe that's..." He trailed off, thoughts whirring.

Michael seemed to understand his floundering, smiling kindly.

"I thought that too," he agreed. "Most mutant children start *showing* abilities around two or three, which later settle about the age we start teaching them. Violet has had hers suppressed all this time; it could very well be messing with her mental layout."

"But?" Ashton pressed, coldness clawing his stomach.

"But it's not the only possibility." Finn yawned into his hand. "I say give her time to get well and truly established here. More lessons, more normalcy. Her brain could work itself out."

"*Could?*"

"That's the other thing." Michael slid his glasses off, inspecting the lenses. He looked tired. "I picked up a rather strange signature from her."

"Signature?" Ashton was beginning to feel like an echo.

"Mm-hm. You could call it a soul, probably the easiest way to explain, but it's *not*. A signature is more like a code. It works *alongside* the soul. Yes, that's more like it. The soul has all the personality and history and details that make us who we are. Our signatures are more to do with our powers, our area or areas of expertise, if you will." Michael pointed at Finn. "He has a healer's signature, it's the core of his abilities."

"What's Vi's? You said she had rare powers, could that be why it's strange?"

"Maybe." Michael laced his fingers, slouching in his seat,

elbows on the arms.

"Uh oh," Finn grimaced.

"Signatures and souls have a weight to them. Not a physical mass, but like a presence. An age. I've not met anyone whose signature and soul weren't the same age."

"Not following."

"Signatures and souls are created in pairs, as the stories go. They can traverse lifetimes together, always together—heard the phrase, 'you've got an old soul'? Yeah, they reincarnate. I think there's something like seven reincarnations before the pair moves on, but that's another story for another time."

Ashton made a mental note of it—what was one more bundle of questions?

Michael rocked in his seat a little. "Vi's soul is her own. But her signature… it felt *old*. Not older, but *old*."

Ash pressed his lips together, fidgeting his hands anxiously. He looked at Finn, to see if he was following this any better, but it didn't appear he was listening. He had picked the book back up, wrinkling his nose as he read.

Michael tipped his head, smiling reassuringly. "Leave it with me. I'll take a gander at it."

"OK," Ashton sighed. "I don't get what this has to do with purple yet though."

"Tally it up," Finn advised, turning the book upside down. Ash saw the text over his shoulder, but it was no longer readable to him.

"What he means," Michael picked up, "is Violet has a number of things against her. First, she's a mutant born to human parents and, yes, she's definitely their daughter, Finn checked her DNA."

"You're welcome," Finn said.

"Second, she has late-stage development powers that are incredibly rare and may seem harmless on the surface, but don't forget what she did to Marlon."

"I won't," Ashton grumbled.

"Third—while she has been here, she has over-exerted herself twice with power usage we would not expect of someone like her, with so little education and preparation."

"Blew up our lights." Finn righted the book and flipped to the first page. "Had to change *all* the bulbs."

"A reaction from a vision." Michael nodded. "That's number four. Five is the purple glow and however she managed to port all the missing, two large rockies, me and herself to the medbay with no prior training."

"Some elementals can travel through their elements, though it's hard to learn and Vi's more of an obscure nature." Finn set the book down, dragging a pen pot to him and turning the contents upside down too, one by one.

Michael laced his fingers, squashing his hands together and glaring wide-eyed at this blatant disrespect to his stationery, but he managed to stay on task for once.

"I do not mean to sound so harsh or judgemental about Violet. She's a very sweet and curious child, just a little lost in the grand scheme of things. But…" He winced. "I do believe she is this purple that will rise."

"But… it—it said prepare for doomsday!" Ashton said.

"Or peace," Michael reminded him. "Peace is an option."

"I'm sure Vi will be fine," Finn said, starting on the next pen pot. Michael snatched the first one back, tipping it out and correcting them in a handful.

Nausea had replaced the cold. Ash met Michael's eyes,

not trusting himself to speak.

"I agree with Finn. I have faith in Violet. Unfortunately, I also know to take heed of these old soothsayers. If they warn it can go either way… we must be wary. It gives no indication of when or how or what or where or anything."

He placed the first pen pot at the opposite end of the desk, away from his pest of a friend. "Vi has much to learn. Let's not tell her about this. She'll only worry," Michael said.

Ash sighed. He couldn't argue with that. To have something like that in one's head… no. It was bad enough she had David lurking about in there, she didn't need anything else.

A knock on the door. Michael didn't even get to call out a welcome, Pepper barging in. She was nothing like the upbeat, take-charge teacher they had left this morning. She was pale, frazzled, hands fretting with her cardigan.

Michael stood, Finn and Ash a split second behind him. "What's wrong?"

"Um…" Pepper pushed her hands through her hair, pulling it taut. "Well, we were porting, as you know. Got a cupcake for you. But, uh…" She glanced at Ashton, tears welling.

His stomach curled.

"Where is she?"

Chapter Twenty

Pepper had never lost a child. *Never*. In all her years of teaching, of *all* the rambunctious young mutants with budding powers and all the chaos that came with them, she had *never* lost one during porting lessons.

For one, she put trackers on them. Two, she had spells in place that stopped them leaving the building. Three, if someone found them, they would bring them straight back, as Finn had the first time Violet ported. There was a good system in place, tried and tested hundreds of times.

Until today.

She and Michael had had a chat about Violet's education, after Leona and everyone had been rescued. He had warned her that things would be different. Not in a dire sense, not outright. Michael, by nature, wanted to better understand Violet, her background, her abilities, her personality, the whole kit and caboodle.

"She's still adjusting to all of this," he had said, "and she's not developed to the normal degree."

"With that man as their dad, could you say *any* of them have?" Pepper asked.

"We have two of them, that's not enough to go by."

"Michael…"

"Rhetorical question. Yep, I see it now. Sorry."

So, Pepper kept an eye on her new pupil. Quiet, shy, clinging to her arm and then trying to sneak out of the room when the other kids came in. Pepper picked her up and sat her in the nearest chair—a direct route to the door, but also an insistence to sit and mingle with children her own age.

Violet looked at no one, keeping her head down. She spoke to no one, not even the girl sitting next to her. Pepper had seated this girl – Taylor – there for a reason; Taylor could coax *anyone* out of their shell.

Taylor introduced herself with a smile. Violet hunched her shoulders, still not looking up. Taylor didn't seem to mind, slinging her coat over the back of her chair.

"Pepper says we're getting cupcakes today." Taylor went on. "I want a red velvet one. My aunt makes the *best* red velvet cake. Have you had red velvet? You should try my aunt's, it's *amazing*." She spread her hands in celebration, grinning. Violet picked at the material of her trouser leg.

Pepper called for the class's attention and the lesson began.

Ten minutes in, Violet's group – they went in fours – came back without her. Pepper didn't even get to ask them where she was, Finn materialising by the desk and grumpily, unceremoniously dropping the girl in the chair there.

"She landed on my *head*," he complained, much to the amusement of the class. He blew a raspberry at them all and left, sulking.

Violet seemed a little perplexed, looking at Pepper.

"It's all right." The teacher comforted with a warm smile. "You're not the first one to land on someone's head and you won't be the last. Ready to keep going?"

Twenty minutes later, the group returned without her again. Taylor and the other two, Idina and Flora, were happily munching on their acquired cupcakes.

Pepper didn't panic then, retrieving her tablet from her desk. See, there was Violet's tracker, in Class Three. She had just missed, easily remedied.

Nope, that was a lie.

Pepper found the tracker – and *just* the tracker – on the desk, blinking its little red light at her as if criticising her for making it wait. She was hesitant to pick it up, scanning the classroom instead. Class Three was still empty at this point. "Violet?" she called, her fingers closing around the tracker. It was just a ball, bouncy ball size, made with a tough plastic outer shell and then whatever made it tick inside. "Violet?" She checked under the tables, checked the storage cupboard at the back, looked out the windows, even opened the drawers of the desk—porting was about space and sometimes that included shrinking effects.

Classes Two, Four and Five were fruitless too. Two and Five were occupied and no one had seen Violet.

So, Pepper expanded her search, taking deep breaths.

"It's OK," she told herself. "She can't have gone far. Someone will bring her in any second now."

She paused, listening in the hallways. "Aaaaaaannnnnyyyy second now. Now. Now. Nnnnnnoooooowwwww..."

Another nope. She waited ten minutes and nothing. An unseen constriction began around her lungs, and she hurried back to Class One, bursting in rather abruptly and interrupting the kids' chatter. She did a quick headcount, but right off the bat, she knew Violet wasn't there—no one else had hair quite so vivid.

That's when she really panicked. She told the kids to stay put, eat their cake, be good, and then dashed from the room, tears scalding her eyes. She ported and landed outside

Michael's door.

Ashton was not happy. *Not* happy. While Finn put the message out over the comms, Ash pestered Michael to port him about. He looked rather green when Pepper dashed past them in the corridor of Floor Three.

"Anything?" he asked.

She shook her head, and he swore under his breath. "Mike, you OK?"

"I'm good. Where do you want to try next?"

"Medbay."

"Kathy said she's not there," Pepper cut in. The message had come through a few minutes ago. "What about your room?"

"First place we checked." Michael rubbed at his temples, squeezing his eyes shut in thought.

"Room, kitchens, gardens, Khaled's, canteen would have called in, not the medbay…"

"None of the classrooms," Pepper added. "Not Floor Two or Floor Three."

"Finn's in my office in case she goes there. Where else—?"

Michael froze. He disappeared, returning in the blink of an eye. "Found her."

"Wh—? Where?"

Michael grabbed their hands and ported them away.

"Oh." Ash croaked. They were back in the cavern; the last one they had found before Violet agreed to go.

He looked up, looked around, seeing rocks, rocks and more rocks. "I hate this place," he mumbled.

Then he saw Violet.

She was sitting cross-legged in the middle of the floor, her back to them. Going by the movements of her arms, she was eating something. Her head was down, watching the floor.

He ran forward, calling her name. She startled, looking over her shoulder, cake crumbs and buttercream icing on her face.

She looked confused to see him, sitting in his relieved hug quietly, puzzling more upon seeing Michael and Pepper.

Ash began fussing over her, holding her face, checking her over for injuries. "Are you OK? What are you doing here?"

She blinked at him, squinting as if he emitted a bright light. "Vi?" he prompted.

"'M OK." She raised her half-eaten cupcake. "Chocolate."

"You were supposed to go back to the classroom," he reminded her gently. "Why didn't you?"

Violet frowned, facing forward again, returning her attention to the floor. He waited a handful of seconds, but her eyes glazed over, thoughts elsewhere. "Oy." He shook her shoulder. "What's so special about the floor?"

"I don't know," she admitted, thumbing a glob of icing off the tip of her nose.

Ashton flicked his focus across the stone floor, giving it a quick study.

"Theeeen, can we leave? I'm not a huge fan of this place. *The walls are watching me,*" he whispered.

Violet hesitated and he repressed a sigh. He was not exaggerating—the immense presence of rock above them was searing the top of his head like a mini, judgemental sun, as if it could read him right down to his soul. Or signature. Or whatever crazy was coming next.

He half-turned to Michael, silently imploring him to help.

Michael and Pepper exchanged glances.

"Go back to your class," he said, touching her arm. "We'll manage from here."

Pepper looked at the siblings nervously but didn't argue. She nodded and ported.

"Violet?" Michael called, walking over on light feet. He crouched next to her too, opposite Ashton. Violet shoved the last of her cake into her mouth, not meeting his gaze. "Something is drawing you here," he noted. "What is it?" Around her mouthful, she managed an 'I-don't-know' noise.

Michael raised an eyebrow at Ashton, who repeated the noise, shrugging. "Helpful," Michael muttered. "Vi, do you need... help here? Do you want me to get one of the rockies?"

She swallowed her cake, wiping crumbs from her T-shirt. "No, thank you."

"I can get Rhonda or Tim. You know them," Michael said.

"No, thank you."

"OK." Michael put his hands on the floor, swinging his legs out to sit cross-legged.

Ash frowned.

"No. Don't do that. Don't get comfortable."

"Ash—"

"Is the air thin down here or is that me?" Ashton laughed, a nervous, panicked sound.

Violet tipped her head at him, examining his face. "I'm OK." He forced a smile. "I'm OK."

"You're lying."

"I am." He nodded, voice an octave or two higher than usual.

Violet winced apologetically.

"What's down here, Vi?" Michael asked.

"I don't know." She repeated, now looking at him. "Something's missing." Michael tilted his head in question. Violet noticed some more crumbs on her shirt, brushing them away too. They scattered across the floor. "There's something missing," she confirmed. "I don't know what. But I need it to figure this out." She tapped a finger on the floor.

"The floor?"

"Yes, yes, everything sticks to the floor because of gravity. Can we go now?" Ash jostled her shoulder.

"I'll get us out of here soon," Michael promised. "What do you need to figure out here?"

Violet shook her head.

"I need the thing first."

"And what's that?"

She looked at him sidelong, biting her lower lip. Michael's mouth tipped in a half-smile. "OK, don't know that either. How—how about we take this up to my office? Before your brother's head explodes." Violet faltered, gaze falling to the floor.

"I'll make you a hot chocolate." Ashton bribed.

"OK," she agreed. Michael held his hands out to each of them, Ashton grabbing on a little too tightly.

They were back in the office in seconds. Finn had occupied Michael's chair in his absence, feet on the desk, crossed at the ankles, lolly in mouth. He waggled his fingers at them, took the sweet out and pointed at Violet with it.

"You," he declared, "are rather troublesome." He paused, contemplating her for a moment. Then he grinned. "I love it. Come work with me."

"Finn—"

"It'll be fun."

"Finn—"

"You can have *all* the lollies you want."

"*Finn!*" Michael smacked his feet from the desk. "First my book, now my desk. Remind me why I'm nice to you."

"You love me."

"In small doses. Move."

"No. You're rude."

"Mm, fine. Excuse me, please."

"Shan't." Finn decided, stubbornly popping his lolly in his mouth and smirking around the stick. Michael fixed an unimpressed look at him. Finn copied, lacing his fingers on his stomach, quite at home there.

That changed when Michael snapped his fingers and brought the return of Finn the Frog, swatting the mouth shut to rub salt in the wound. From somewhere inside, Finn's muffled wails of protest.

"Sorry, what was that? I don't speak Ribbit."

Finn muttered something undoubtedly rude but blissfully kept in the frog head and disappeared. Michael grinned victoriously and sank into the chair that was rightfully his. "Ew, he's made it all warm. Take a seat, you two."

"I'm seriously considering setting up camp in here." Ash remarked. Michael laughed, leaning back in his chair, resting his elbow on the arm.

"Yes, that would make it easier to keep an eye on you both."

He turned his chair a fraction, tilting his head at Violet. "So, what do you need and what's missing?"

She shrugged a shoulder.

Michael adjusted his glasses. "Is it anything we can get?" She shook her head, picking at her T-shirt. "Is it anything you've seen while here?"

Another no.

Michael bit his lip, sifting through his thoughts.

Ash leant over.

"We can't help if you don't tell us."

"But I don't know," she insisted. "I just... I just know something's missing and—and I need it to figure out..." She trailed off, brow furrowing.

For a moment, she was quiet, battling to find a way around her confusion. Ash and Michael waited patiently, although they did share a look to see if the other was making sense of this. That was not the case.

Sniffles brought them back, tears welling in her eyes. Michael summoned a box of tissues and Ashton scooted his chair closer, gently placing his hand on her arm.

She was apologising before he even got a chance to speak, croaking and sobbing. Michael gathered a wad of tissues and leant across the desk to pass them to her.

"Vi, what—? Why are you crying?"

"I— I don't kn-know, I'm s-s-sorry."

"You don't need to apologise for not knowing something," Michael reassured her.

She shook her head, clumping the tissues under her eyes. "We just want to help, but we need you on board to do that. If you're not ready—"

"Man," she coughed.

Michael tensed. When he next spoke, his tone was not as light or comforting, but guarded, wary.

"What man?" Violet pulled her arm from under Ash's hand and pointed. At first, Ashton thought she was pointing at *him*. But when Michael looked past him, he realised, turning in his seat.

"He's there," she said, still pointing.

Ash couldn't see anyone and going by the grimace on Michael's face, he didn't either. Without looking around, he pushed his sister's hand down.

"How long have you been seeing this man, Vi?" Michael asked, still staring at the space she had indicated. Violet began fiddling with her tissues, sniffing.

"Milk," she replied, barely audible. Michael nodded, as if having expected that answer.

"What does he look like?" Ash didn't want to get involved – he had seen the films – but he had to ask. He didn't much like when she hesitated.

"I don't know. He… he doesn't have a face."

"Oh, joy." Ashton laughed uneasily. "Have you got insurance on this place, Mike? I'm gonna burn it down."

"Please don't," Michael sighed. He opened the top left drawer, retrieving a pad of paper and colouring pencils. "Draw him for me," he slid the items across the surface to Violet, "please."

"Is he dead?" Ash asked. "Was he summoned? Was he trapped in an heirloom or an artefact or a hidden basement?"

"Ashton…" Michael warned.

"Na-uh. I know how this works. I ain't dying today, no sir!"

"He wants to show me something," Violet said, studying her pencils.

She picked black to begin with, sketching a wobbly outline of a man. A long coat buttoned to his throat, trousers tucked into his boots, messy hair and, yep, no face. Ash watched her draw with trepidation, though he *did* like that coat—very suave.

She tipped the colours out onto the desk, picking a dark purple. Ash saw Michael wince and slouch in his chair.

"What does he want to show you?"

"I don't know. He kept pointing at the floor."

"In the cavern?"

She nodded, pouting when her brother leant over to tell her to crosshatch.

"Does he speak to you?" Michael asked.

"No. He hasn't got a mouth."

"How do you know what he wants then?"

"Can feel it."

She finished colouring the coat, ignoring Ashton's hissing at messiness—white patches, over the lines, colouring at different angles—and picked the black pencil up again, starting on the trousers. When she passed over the line between trousers and boots without a second thought, she was sure Ash's head was *really* going to explode this time. "I am being *quick*," she told him.

"You are *hurting* me."

"I am not artsy."

"I can see that," he muttered. She stuck her tongue out at him, still scribbling. "Does he have a name?"

"Not that I know."

"Is he still standing behind me?" Ash kept his tone as carefree as he could, but his mind was firing away for any form of attack against a faceless ghost. Violet paused her colouring to look up quickly.

"Yes." She nodded and went back to her drawing.

"Does he, uh, *have* to stand behind me?"

"Yes."

"Great. Cool. Love that. Michael—"

"Arson is still a no."

"You didn't even consider it!" Ash complained.

Michael met his gaze, raising an eyebrow.

"I grew up with Finn. I live with pyromaniacs. I manage mutants who think arson is a fun prank. It has been well considered for a long time and my answer remains unchanged."

"Mmph. Funsponge."

"Done," Violet announced, sliding the notepad back to Michael.

He picked it up, holding it in both hands and effectively hiding himself from view.

"Does he have any colours?"

"No. No lines either."

"Have you seen anyone else like that?"

"No."

They could see the top of Michael's hair bob as he nodded. He remained quiet, concentrating on the picture. Violet leant in her seat, tapping her brother's arm. "You OK?"

"Oh, for sure. Devil Stairs in a mutant stronghold with a faceless man standing behind me that only you can see." He nodded seriously. "If that doesn't kill me, I don't know what will."

"He won't kill you." Violet looked past him inquisitively. "I think he likes you."

"Ha," he croaked. "Ha-ha, that's *grand*. Michael—"

"No arson. No flooding. No demolition."

"What about—?"

"No, we're not relocating."

"Exorcism?"

"Those don't work here."

"*Why?*" Ashton protested. "Vi says he likes me, which means I'm lined up to be a sacrifice!"

Michael lowered the drawing, revealing his eyes. "Don't look at me like that." Ash protested. "I *know* how these things work!"

"Violet. You broke your brother."

"Sorry."

Michael put the drawing down, straightening his glasses.

"I don't recognise anything about this man. I've not heard of a faceless man haunting this place either."

"Oh, sweet Lord." Ash slumped in his chair. "What else is there?"

"Mm. Ask Kathy. She's part of a little group that studies them."

"So, you can't have exorcisms, but you can have paranormal hunting parties?"

"Yes. Glad you're finally getting it." Michael smiled lopsidedly. "Vi, why doesn't he have a face?"

She gaped at him. Michael winced. "That came out ruder than I intended. Sorry. Sorry," he said to the empty space that wasn't really empty behind Ashton.

"I don't know," she said. "But it's... I think it's like someone wanted him forgotten."

Ash hissed, displeased, and sinking more in his chair. Violet glanced over. The man's head was bowed, watching Ash with an air of bemusement, hands tucked behind his back.

Michael pulled her drawing pad back to him, tearing the picture off and placing it to one side. He picked up a pencil and began jotting down notes on the fresh page.

"Forgotten, why? By whom? Who would want him

forgotten?"

Violet hunched her shoulders.

Ash had now slid down to the floor and was crawling past her, between her and the desk, and coming up the other side of her.

"I'm going to get that hot chocolate," he decided. "Mike, is there holy water anywhere? Or a cross? Silver bullets? Wooden stake? Do I need to remove the head?"

"I'll have some tea please, Ash. Eight sugars."

"You're so weird," Ash muttered, hurrying from the room.

"Likewise," Michael said happily. "Your brother is a funny one."

Violet nodded in agreement.

The man moved to sit in Ash's empty seat, folding one leg over the other and placing his hands in his lap neatly. Michael looked up. "Any idea why you can see him and no one else?" She shook her head, biting her lip.

Michael tapped his pencil on the paper, peering at her curiously. "What is it?"

"He, um… I think he made you say about my training." Michael's brow creased.

Violet hesitated, but then recounted the man's sudden appearance in their room, after Ashton threw the tablet pinning the blame of their mum's death on her. When she spoke of the man touching Michael's shoulder, his hand strayed to it.

"I thought I felt something. It was…cool and tingly, but… I just wanted to get you to class, I didn't even question it."

Michael looked at where the man had been standing, Violet correcting him with a point. He stared at Ashton's chair, puzzling and twisting his pencil between his fingers. "I take it he led you through the caverns too?" She nodded. "And when we found you, just now, was he there?"

She nodded again.

Michael bit the end of his pencil, thinking. "Does he come and go as he pleases, or does he turn up at certain times or—?" He rolled his hand, leaving space for suggestions.

"First one, I think."

The door opened and Ash was back, carrying a tray of three steaming mugs, an entire packet of custard creams and an entire packet of chocolate digestives.

Michael waved his hand, summoning another chair. Ash raised an eyebrow at it as he set the tray on the desk.

"On your feet, lose your seat." Michael advised, gesturing with his pencil to Ashton's old chair.

"He stole my chair?"

"Yep."

"Oooh, why me?" He plopped in the new chair and tore open the custard creams.

"You can handle mutants, but not ghosts?"

"I can *see* mutants. They make *sense*. Or more sense than ghosts anyway." He scrunched his nose disapprovingly, settling into a sulky silence.

Michael turned a laugh into a cough.

Violet looked to her left. It was still rather difficult, but she was sure the man was watching Ashton. She didn't feel there was anything to worry about; Ash simply entertained him, something she sensed the man had been lacking.

His head turned and she could feel his attention fall on her. He inclined his head, his hand gripping her forearm. Michael's office fell away, engulfed by purple splotches of all different shades, pulsing and splattering in slow motion all around her. The effect made her woozy, but it only lasted a couple of seconds. She blinked and was back in a room.

Not the office. Iron bands crushed her ribs, pressing down on her lungs. Ice and lava collided in her blood. She was still sitting, but not in the comfy chair she had been.

She was back in the basement, back in the old seat, held in place by unseen forces as she was every time David brought her down here.

A scream built in her throat but progressed no further. Her hands would not move, her legs as equally compliant.

The basement was not as she had last seen it. The monitors were smashed, a hammer – *the* hammer – still embedded in one. The supplies in and on the desks had been thrown, swept up in a hurricane of rage and hate, now all over the floor in trampled, torn, smashed, ruined states.

Look.

The word spiked into her mind, a calm man's voice she did not recognise, but knew who it belonged to. *Look*, the man insisted, *it is here.*

What is?

Look.

She *was* looking. Everything had been decimated, she was paralysed, the basement was only a few shades away from complete darkness. She could move her eyes and nothing else, the air shimmering to her left. The man appeared, a faint image of him, still faceless, partially see-through. He raised his arm, pointing. She followed his direction to the stairs. The door was shut, no light coming from above, but that wasn't what he wanted her to look at.

Something *below* the stairs. That made no sense, it was a solid wall beneath the steps...

"Violet!"

Her eyes snapped open, inhaling sharply. Ash was shaking her by the shoulders, panic-stricken. Michael was still on the other side of the desk, examining her from behind a book.

Ash shook her again. "Vi! Vi? Can you hear me? Are you OK? What happened?"

"Let her breathe, Ash."

"No! She can breathe when she stops glowing and giving me a heart attack! *Violet!*"

"Ashton!"

"Oh good, your brain still works." He let her go, poking her in the forehead. "I think. Are you all right?"

The man was still sitting next to her, as nonchalant as he had been before, as if nothing had happened.

Her heart had apparently been tied to a jackhammer. Her chest hurt, as though someone had gathered her organs up in one of those machines that crushed things down. Looking down at her hands, she saw nothing of this glow Ashton was on about, but she could feel the after-effects of it, like she had just stepped out of a warm bath.

Michael lowered his book, having been using it as a shield, frowning worriedly.

"I'll get Finn," he said, disappearing before either sibling could say anything.

"Vi?" Ash took her hand, gently squeezing it between both of his upon feeling her shaking. "What is it? Did you see something?"

She nodded, neck stiff.

"What? Are the others—?"

"I didn't see them."

An odd look of relief and concern crossed his face.

She hadn't seen their brothers and sisters this time, but

were they OK? Had David done anything to them?

Michael returned, Finn – now frogless – at his side.

"What have you done now?" he demanded, hands on hips. "Honestly, can't leave you alone for five minutes."

"Finn—"

"Right, right." The medic held his hands up innocently, coming around the desk. "Let's have a look at you then."

The man shifted next to her. Violet started, trying to call up a warning, but he was quicker. He shot forward in his seat, hand splaying against Finn's chest. The medic gasped, doubling over as though the strike was more than physical.

"Finn!" Michael was there in an instant, catching his friend as he staggered back. "What—? Finn? *Finn?*"

The man sat back, folding his arms.

Violet stared at him, numbness creeping through her limbs. She then looked from him to Michael, tears brimming in his eyes as his friend hung limply in his hold, head lolling. "Finn!"

Finn did not answer, staring at the floor, eyes unseeing. Michael jostled him, crying, "*Finn!*"

To be continued...